THE EAGLE HAS FALLEN

THE EAGLE HAS FALLEN

P A Lemos

ATHENA PRESS
LONDON

THE EAGLE HAS FALLEN
Copyright © P A Lemos 2004

All Rights Reserved

ISBN 1 84401 315 4

First Published in 2004 by
ATHENA PRESS
Queen's House, 2 Holly Road
Twickenham TW1 4EG
United Kingdom

Printed for Athena Press

One

Sailor turned Senator

It was very quiet in the little cove of this remote Greek island. The sea was calm and there was no wind. It was springtime and the only sounds one could hear were the birds on the two isolated fig trees.

The only sign of human life was a neat, whitewashed little church at the top of the hill.

On the right side coming into the cove, there were vineyards all the way up the slope of the small hills, and towards the sea there was a line of pine trees. On the left side there was a huge settlement of fisheries or fish farms and one could see the nets that divide the varying types of fish.

Outside the little church there were beautiful wild flowers, a lovely variation of yellow, white and pink. One could tell that at this time of the year the flowers were blooming, and their perfume was overwhelming.

The stillness was abruptly interrupted when a very fast speedboat approached the little cove from the sea. There was only one person at the helm. The craft approached, reduced speed, and the driver berthed the craft alongside the little wooden jetty. He tied the boat up and jumped out, and rather in a hurry, he headed in the direction of the little church.

He stopped outside for a second, looked around, pushed the door open and disappeared inside.

From the direction of the sea came a small wooden boat; there were two men inside working the oars. They approached the wooden jetty, moored the little boat, and one of the men jumped out and started climbing the narrow street towards the little church. The other untied the boat and started moving out to sea, westwards.

Two people, a young man and his girl, were witnessing these movements and they could not understand the whole thing. What would those two people be doing in a deserted little church on such a small, isolated island?

'Do you think they are spies?' the girl asked.

'Don't be silly – what would spies do in this part of the world?' the young man reassured her.

At this very moment, a dilapidated old motor car appeared on the road leading to a lighthouse. There was only one person in the car. He approached the little church, stopped and got out. He looked around, noticed the speedboat that was still tied to the mole and went inside the little church.

'So, now there are three,' said the girl.

'Wait a little. They may become four or even five.'

There was stillness and quietness. The wind started becoming fresher, and as the young man watched the sea towards the west, he saw the same little rowing boat approaching the little wooden jetty. He noticed that there was one passenger and he realised that he was rather tall, blond and had the aristocratic features of the Viking people.

This man jumped out of the little boat and, like the others, he started off in the direction of the little church. When he arrived there, the door was opened by somebody inside, who looked as if he was welcoming a late arrival.

'I think we should report this to the police when we get back to the village. They may know what is going on,' said the girl in a hushed voice.

'Let me investigate first with the port authority, where there's a friend of mine. I will drop by this evening and ask if they know of any strangers who wanted to do a "memorial service" in the little church.'

Inside the church, four men were sitting around a small, round table. The blond man who had arrived last spoke.

'We are all here. We have a proxy from No.3 who could not attend our meeting. I am afraid I have bad news from No.3. He was diagnosed with cancer and he is going through a rather painful course of radiotherapy.' He paused. 'There are two matters we have to discuss: one is whether we go on with supporting Mr X for the US Presidential Elections in November; and the other is whether we should liquidate the person in charge of the terrorist organisation that has been terrorising Greek society for the last twenty years.

'You have in front of you two sheets of paper explaining the two items, giving details and names. You have ten minutes to study these, and then we should vote.'

There were small discussions between the others and after the ten minutes, the blond man, No.1, got up and said, 'First item: elections in US. Do we support Mr X?'

All three lifted their hands in approval.

'Okay,' said No.1, 'the motion is carried. Second item: the liquidation of the man behind the terrorist organisation.'

Again all three lifted their hands in approval.

'Okay, okay. You will authorise me to proceed on my own with both items, as in previous cases, and I will have to report to you in the usual way, through the usual channels of communication.' He looked at them.

'No need to remind you that on leaving here, you will have to proceed in the same way we normally do with a twenty-minute interval between each one of you leaving.'

The chris-craft was still moored at the wooden mole. The blond man approached, jumped inside and started doing something inside the craft. He was bent over for about twenty minutes arranging the ropes and some electric wires. When he'd finished, he untied the boat and pushed it in the direction of the open sea. The boat went along without anybody driving it. It went about one hundred metres, and suddenly, without warning, a small explosion occurred. Within seconds the chris-craft split open and sank, all in small pieces.

The young couple saw the four men all leaving at regular intervals, without giving any indication as to where they came from.

'I thought that we were going to have a lovely quiet romantic afternoon, but these unusual events have spoiled everything,' said the young man.

'Never mind,' the girl said. 'We will have other times together but... but this is most unusual, and very intriguing, don't you think?'

The young man enquired with his friend at the port office. He went to the police, and he even asked the fishermen who worked around the island, but nobody saw anybody. Nobody saw or heard of the speedboat, or the car, or the rowing boat. It was all a mystery!

★

At the house of the prospective Senator for the State of New York, all the family gathered.

Michael Glinos was very anxious to hear the election result, which was going to be declared about midnight; although he felt inside him that he would win. He had worked so hard since the time he decided to leave the shipping company that was his life and start his political career.

It was not an easy decision. Being in shipping, being the Managing Director of a large shipping company, was more to his taste, closer to his heart. He has seen difficult years and good years, but on the whole the company that had been founded by his great-grandfather was well established, and it had gone from strength to strength. He has also seen bad years, with a crisis in shipping. He remembered once he walked into the office of the Chairman of the Marine and National Bank with the intention of telling him that the bank could have all their ships because the fleet was working at a loss.

'What can we do with thirty ships?' the Chairman asked Michael. 'If you cannot make any money out of these ships, nobody else will. Anyway,' the Chairman continued, 'go on for another six months and we'll talk again then. Meanwhile, we will support your company so that you can run your ships.'

Michael was reminiscing while he was in his study, waiting for the results. His family – his wife and children, his brother and sister – were still at the table enjoying the beautiful lobsters he had bought from the Long Island shop of a friend of his.

He was going over his life, from the time he started as a young Captain in the company, his voyages both in cargo ships and oil tankers and hundreds of incidents he'd experienced in various ports around the world.

The whole family wanted him to go into politics. They all thought that one of the family should 'escape' ships and the sea and become a Senator – or who knows, even President of the USA. The only person who did not really want him to go into politics was Michael himself. He was absolutely and utterly in love with the sea; but... but the ancient Greek philosophers used to say: 'Many people dislike wealth, but nobody dislikes glory.'

The family, and especially his wife, Amalia, finally won the argument. Michael committed himself deeply to politics. Of course he had all the necessary qualifications and attributes. He was hard working, he loved people, he was charitable, and he was also very, very handsome.

As he was sipping his coffee in his study, he started remembering…

He was back in Yokohama on board a bulk carrier. He was the chief officer and they were discharging coal. He'd just come on board from the office of the stevedores and knew that within one hour the discharge would be completed and they had to sail straight away.

He asked the officer on watch, 'Where is the Captain?'

'The Captain? Forget it. The Captain has not appeared on board since yesterday evening.' And of course the way the officer said this indicated that the Captain was nowhere to be found.

Michael knew that the Captain, in spite of his long experience and good seamanship, was a womaniser; and the moment the ship was in port, the Captain would disappear into the red-light district; and Yokohama was famous for its red-light district.

Michael called a taxi. He authorised the second Officer to supervise the cargo's discharge and went straight towards the bars and brothels at the seafront. After one hour of painstaking search, he finally found a Mamasan who told him, 'Yes, yes, the nice Greek Captain is upstairs! He is okay: he gave a lot of money to my girls, but now he is asleep.'

Within minutes, Michael and the Captain, who was still not sober, were on their way to the ship.

Then he remembered another incident in Rotterdam when he was now a Captain of a cargo ship and they were just finishing cargo work. At that moment the new chief engineer, with two seamen, arrived on the speedo to join the ship.

He allowed the chief half an hour to settle in his room and then went down to welcome him.

'Welcome, Chief. I am afraid you will not have a lot of time to familiarise yourself with the engine room, but they

told me from Piraeus that you are an experienced engineer…'
And so on.

'Okay, okay, Captain. All this is not important. What is important is my fine collection of pipes, smoking pipes. I brought twelve of them some from Scotland, some from Lebanon and—'

The Captain intervened. 'Chief, we are sailing in an hour. We have to check our bunkers and prepare the engines and…'

The chief engineer stopped the Captain with a gesture meaning that he was not interested in preparing the ship for the voyage. He said, 'Captain, bear in mind that if we get to an English port I have to meet the representative of Dunhill, who make the best pipes in the world.'

'*Chief!*' the Captain shouted. 'Chief, stop talking about pipes and let's talk about the ship and our voyage to the USA.'

'No, Captain. I am sure you have full instructions from the office about the voyage, so all I am concerned about is showing you my collection of pipes. Nothing else.'

'Okay, Chief, wait here a minute. I will be back in five minutes.'

The Captain then rushed to the cabin of the second engineer, an elderly man with fifty years' experience at sea as an engineer. He virtually shouted, 'Nicola, can you take over as Chief from now until the pilot joins us off Baltimore? Then I will have a new chief engineer.'

'Of course, Captain Michael. For years I have practically run the engine room of this ship. No problem.'

The Captain disappeared back to the chief engineer's cabin.

'Chief, you are going back home. I will arrange with the agent to send you back to Piraeus tomorrow morning. And there… there you can take care of your famous pipes.'

'What do you mean? What is the meaning of this?' the chief complained.

'Nothing, Chief. You are simply dismissed. You are no good for my ship.'

And with these words, the Captain rushed to his office to phone the agent about the repatriation of the newly arrived chief engineer.

At this moment the phone rang next to his desk. It was from his company's office, his assistant.

'Sir, we are going ahead. Gallup and exit polls predict a 60% win for you. Do you hear that, sir, Mr Senator?'

His reveries were interrupted and Michael was back to reality.

'Okay, okay. Keep me advised every hour.'

They were beautiful years, rewarding years, he thought. Rotterdam held so many memories. Then he remembered how once he was chief officer of a car carrier and they were berthing in Waalhaven.

It was about midnight, it was raining hard and he was arranging the ropes and anchors.

A girlfriend he had in Rotterdam had phoned him and promised to wait for him at the quay to take him away for... for a good time.

So he dressed up quickly, shaved and when the stevedores put up a ladder, he was the first to go down, only to see waiting at the berth the shipowner, Captain Stefanos, and the girlfriend.

The shipowner realised the situation and shouted to him, 'Where are you going when the ship is hardly berthed?' He was speechless. 'Okay, you're dismissed. We need no chief officer like you.'

'Sir,' Michael protested, 'I will be back on board in an hour.'

'No!' Stefanos shouted. 'You have to choose. Either you go back on board or you go out with this nice young lady.'

Before Captain Stefanos finished his words, the chief officer had said goodnight to the girl and was halfway up the ladder, back on the ship.

He had some lucky escapes when he was a Captain.

They had a charter of three consecutive voyages of scrap metal from the United States to Western Italy, including Sicily.

They arrived in Palermo for the discharge of the first cargo and they were offloading the cargo extremely slowly. Twenty days had gone by and only half the cargo was taken. Michael was desperate, and as the cargo went down in the hold, it became more difficult to discharge. The New York office was anxious to find a solution.

One evening when he was in the ship's office, two nicely-dressed men in very dark suits and black ties appeared and said to Michael, 'Captain, your discharge is very slow. What are you going to do?'

Silence from Michael. The dark-complexioned man continued, 'We can finish the cargo in five days' time. We run the stevedores, the port authorities; in fact we run everything.'

Michael jumped at him.

'How can you do this? What bonus do you want from me or the owners of the ship?'

'No bonus; no bonus at all. All you will have to do is to take with you to Baltimore two packets weighing about 50kg each. Also from Baltimore you will allow our friends to convey by your ship 100 boxes of cigarettes and 100 boxes of whiskey.'

Michael started to get the idea. He asked the men to allow him until tomorrow to think and to reply.

Next morning, the same two men arrived early.

Michael had discussed the matter with the office in New York and the boss told him to exercise his judgement and decide for himself. But in no way he should take the 50kg of drugs.

'Gentlemen,' he said to the Mafiosi, 'I will bring you the cigarettes and whiskey but... but in no way I will take the drugs to the USA.'

Without reply the two men left the ship. They had promised to reply to the Captain the next day.

The Captain did not know what to do because the Mafiosi did not come back. He noticed, however, that the cargo was getting out of the ship very quickly.

The day before he sailed, he received a phone call from one of the men. He said to him, 'Captain, you are an honourable man. We will help you. Maybe next trip you will help us.'

It was after two-thirty when there was a knock on his door and his wife rushed in. She embraced him and said, 'Congratulations, Mr Senator! You made it my love. You made it!'

'Actually,' Michael said, 'we made it, because it was due to your perseverance and hard work that I won. The only trouble is that we have to move to Washington DC and leave our beautiful apartment here in New York, and our country house in White Plains.'

At that moment everybody who had been in the next room – some manning the telephone lines, some employees of the shipping company, some relations, and Michael's two children – rushed in to congratulate him.

'What does a Senator do?' enquired his young daughter.

Her brother jumped at her. '"What does a Senator do?" How can you be so stupid? What do they teach you at school? How to kill people and the use of guns and all the terrible things we hear about? You are supposed to know about the Constitution of the US, about the Administration – all about these things.'

'Okay, okay, bighead! I know what Senators do. But, but I wanted to hear it from Dad. I am very proud of our dad.'

Two

Cruising into Danger

On a mountain slope, high up in Afghanistan, a training course was being held. In fact, they were training for sabotage and terrorism and the two weapons specialists – the 'professors', as they all called them – were tough and extremely strict.

'This is a serious training course you are going through. It is not for ordinary war methods. This is for sabotage and the serious killing of our enemies; for the enemies of our brothers and for the enemies of democratic principles. It is not sufficient to go on protest marches and shout that we are against the brutal USA and that we are against world domination by the capitalists! Our task is to show them in deeds and actions what we mean. And we mean to kill, to assassinate the enemies of the people. This is the only language the capitalists understand!'

And after saying all this, one of the 'professors' gave a long diatribe about explosives and described in great detail the use of several explosives, from the usual Semtex to the more powerful explosives used by the suicide bombers belonging to Hamas and the other terrorist organisations in the Middle East.

The young American and his girlfriend were listening very carefully. They had arrived there two weeks ago after deciding that life in the USA or in Europe was not for them.

They had decided that they did not agree with the general theory and life as it is lived in the West. They did not agree with the horrible actions of the CIA and the FBI and the double standards of the Administration.

It had all started when the two of them were studying at the university in Boston. Young Makis was hesitant in the beginning, but under the strong influence of his girlfriend, who was studying politics, he was persuaded that *'they were living in a rotten society and that soon the river that is called public demand will destroy and drown the capitalistic world'*.

Mary-Clare had her roots in a very poor family from Gary, Indiana, and was extremely bitter. Her affection for Makis and her twisted attitude about life created a sort of violent attraction that made him put aside his principles and the family teaching he received at home. In time he decided that Mary-Clare's attitudes and her extreme stance toward society were correct.

Makis had a lot of problems at home because neither his father nor his mother agreed with his revolutionary ideals. In fact, one night when he appeared home at about four o'clock in the morning, there was a violent argument and his father told him in so many words, 'I have two other children to think about and I do not wish them to have ideals as per Mao Tse-tung!'

That was the final rift, and subsequently Makis was fully under the influence of his girl, who declared to him one day that the best thing for them would be to leave the USA and go to the Taleban territory or some other place where the Mujaheddin would train them as revolutionaries, in which case they would be able to serve 'the people'.

They had several discussions; they even parted for a month or so because Makis was not convinced that they should abandon everything – their families and their friends – and go to be trained as revolutionaries and killers in the mountains of Afghanistan. In fact, Makis was of the opinion that by remaining in the West and expressing their revolutionary views among the students or the ordinary people, the results would be more satisfactory. He had even agreed to be involved in some sort of sabotage or similar acts of negative business, just to show to the capitalist world of theirs that 'the people will not remain inactive any more'.

Finally, they both agreed to spend a couple of months in Palestine, where they could be involved in the struggle against the Jews, against society, against everybody… against the world.

It was not a difficult step to go from Palestine to the wilderness of Afghanistan and to become involved with the Taleban and the indoctrination of terrorism and destruction.

The surroundings were beautiful. Although the general view from their hut was a bit wild and the mountains were rather bare, the training ground was rather pleasant and it had all the amenities for a useful and pleasant stay. There was a recreation building, but on the whole everything was grim and austere, and it all smelt of death and suicide.

When the couple received their orders to proceed to the USA to commit certain acts of terrorism and sabotage, Makis had second thoughts. That evening, after dinner, he had his first serious argument with his girl. This lasted for a few hours and still at the end Makis was not convinced.

'How can we go and kill innocent people? Okay, I understand that we can blow up a house or a bridge, or even explode a train or a boat; but killing ordinary people in a supermarket or on a bus is beyond my understanding.'

'You are not a true revolutionary! You are probably yellow. I do not see how I really believed in you and spent years of my life teaching you and indoctrinating you,' Mary-Clare replied.

They'd been told, 'Your orders are that you will proceed to the USA and there you will receive specific instructions from one of the USA cells, and you are to absolutely execute their wishes. If for some reason you fail to carry out our orders, you give us all the authority to deal with you in any way we decide, even to the extent of executing you for the benefit of the struggle of the people.'

The next morning, one of their 'professors' called them and asked them to present themselves for an indoctrination class.

They were only the two of them, and Makis was slightly afraid. He could not think of the reason for their being asked 'to discuss the future of their careers'.

The professor came in, and without great discussion he told them that 'they were not yet ready for the ultimate sacrifice, not yet ready to undertake suicide attacks, and that they would be sending them North to another camp for further indoctrination and training.'

And within two hours, they were loaded on a dilapidated old truck and were on their way to the unknown. Not even the knowledgeable Mary-Clare knew where they were heading.

Makis tried to ask one of the drivers where they were going. Either the driver was deaf or he just did not want to communicate. The girl started being nasty and serious. She told Makis that he was not up to the standards of a terrorist and she doubted whether the 'professors' would ever give him a serious job to carry out with explosives and so on...

★

There was a big party, a house-warming party, at the new house of Senator Michael. Everybody was present, including the Vice President of the United States.

The house was in a fashionable suburb of Washington DC, and the new Senator had his family with him; his wife, his son and daughter, as well as his brother and sister, and of course the whole of the political Party organisation. In addition there were several members of the shipping company who formed the basis of the Senators organisation.

The best of Washington DC's caterers were engaged, and in addition to the champagne and drinks and canapés there were an abundance of Greek mezes and excellent lobster and shrimp.

Senator Mike was in conversation with a member of his organisation who belonged to the Party, and was a member of the Foreign Affairs Committee.

'Senator, I am afraid the news is bad. We have had confirmation that your cousin, Makis, has disappeared with a girl, and we've had confirmation from our CIA contacts from the Middle East that he has gone East, possibly to Afghanistan. We do not know why or for what purpose, but from a friend of his at the university, we heard that he was becoming an extremist, that he was inclined to be a revolutionary, and his favourite expression was, "We cannot go against the flood that is called popular wish or need" – or words to this effect.'

'Okay, enough said,' replied the Senator. It appeared that he was clearly worried. 'Continue to follow Makis' movements. Spare no effort, spare no expense, but do not forget: all is confidential – fully confidential – and nothing is to appear in our political scene. A scandal like this could ruin our organisation and my chances in the Senate. I will speak to Makis' father tomorrow, to see how they are dealing with this – this terrible tragedy.'

The Senator went straight to the library where the majority leader, the Chairman of the Foreign Affairs Committee, as well as two staunch supporters of the Party, were discussing current topics – which were 'dealing with terrorism', and of course the Budget appropriations.

'We congratulate our new Senator for New York. Not only has he brought new blood into our ranks, but he also comes from a family that fought for the USA, a family with old roots in shipping, and also I understand the Senator was in the USA Navy. He served in the Far East, in the Pacific and in Vietnam.'

'Sir, you are overestimating my worth. I did my duty in the navy and I come from a family that had a lot of interests in shipping and I am originally of Greek origin.'

At that moment Michael's wife, Amalia, came in and interrupted the conversation.

'Gentlemen, you have deserted us! Please come in so that we can all have the benefit of your conversation and wisdom.'

'Only wives have wisdom,' one of the elderly Senators interjected. 'Anyway, we should join the ladies.'

The evening went on and there was music and excellent food. However, Michael could not enjoy the occasion because he was thinking of the news he'd heard about his distant relation.

*

The time passed quickly in the high mountain camp where Makis and Mary-Clare were taken. The teaching there was purely for hard-core revolutionaries. They were taught the use of guns and especially explosives of all different types; and of course, the idea of self-sacrifice and of using themselves as sacrificial entities was introduced and fully exploited.

Naturally Makis did not really like the idea that he should die or sacrifice himself for the benefit of the 'people' or the organisation. One night he had another violent argument with his girlfriend, who was well and truly convinced by the idea of kamikaze-type operations.

Makis was following the indoctrination lessons and procedures without real conviction, and after a few weeks he started thinking how he could possibly get out of this organisation.

Towards the end of the season, he was summoned, together with his girlfriend, for an important session with the top men of the camp.

'Your next assignment is the hijacking of a large cruise

ship. We will not give you more details, for security reasons. You will proceed to a Pakistani port where the cruise liner is scheduled to call and you will get instructions there. You may have to "liquidate" the Captain, the chief officer and chief engineer, and get assistance from two of our own revolutionaries who are already on board. Any questions?'

'Yes. I have a few questions,' Makis declared.

'They'd better be good, your questions, because you have shown signs of weakness,' came the reply.

'Why do we have to kill ordinary seamen like the Captain, the chief officer and the chief engineer? They are ordinary people. What is the purpose of the hijacking? Do we get any benefit from this activity? Will the people – the ordinary people of the world – get any real benefit?'

'You will be excused completely from this assignment. Your heart is not in the real purpose of our organisation. You had better disappear completely, and bear in mind that if we find out that you have opened your mouth or that you uttered one word as to where we are, who we are and what we are doing, then… then your life will not be worth a penny. Do you understand fully?'

The man glared at him, then went on, 'The girl stays. She is okay. She is well and truly, passionately ours. She is indoctrinated.'

He stopped for a moment. He called two guards outside and told them, 'This man should stay here under house arrest. I will tell you when you can release him and where he will be sent.'

Mary-Clare tried to reason with the boss but her protests were completely unsuccessful.

Finally the man asked in a loud, stern voice, 'Are you part of us? Will you go to this assignment for the hijacking of the cruise ship, or do you want to stay here with your man? He is not revolutionary material. You know that!'

After a few moments' hesitation and after talking to

Makis, who was on his way out with the two guards, Mary-Clare said to the boss, 'I am with you. I should not buckle and let my feelings govern my decisions and overrule my revolutionary teachings.' She pursed her lips.

'…No, no. We go together, Mujaheddin,' she continued. 'I will be responsible for Makis. We will be a team for the cruise ship affair. Please, accept my word. And if I see a sign of weakness, any sign that Makis will not fulfil our orders, I promise that I will immediately execute him.'

'Are you sure of his devotion to the cause, and his devotion to you?' the Mujaheddin shouted at her.

'Yes, yes! I swear, I will execute him!'

The cruise ship *Sea of Galilee* was approaching her moorings in the outer port of Karachi. The sea was calm and there was a light rain which made visibility rather poor. Captain Joseph, with his two senior officers, were on the bridge. They had just given four forward ropes to the tugs that approached them from the direction of the port.

This would be the last trip for old Joseph. He had bought a nice house in Scotland, where he came from; he had spent a lot of his money redecorating it and improving the garden, and he was looking forward to his well-deserved retirement and life at home with his wife, his daughter and her family, as he was basically lazy.

He was looking forward to becoming a member of the local Yacht Club, even a member of the committee.

The chief engineer, an old Scottish seadog who had started his career just after the War, was pleased with the performance of the engines, the generators, the air-conditioning units and in fact with practically everything; and although there was a list of 120 small complaints in the records of the two superintendents who were travelling with them, on the whole, the voyage was uneventful. After all, it was the first voyage of this luxurious cruise ship.

There were 1,500 passengers on board: Americans, Europeans who had boarded in Italy, and a number of Arabs who'd come on board in Alexandria and Jedda.

The two Greek superintendents were discussing the list of defects. They of course realised that most of them came from difficult, neurotic passengers, who were upset because a pipe was vibrating or a steel beam was not properly welded, or the mirror in the bathroom showed the lady to be more fat than she was actually, or the air-conditioning fan was noisy.

The superintendents had had a hard time. Some of the passengers were demanding and really difficult.

There was the case of an elderly lady from Palm Beach who insisted that one of the beams in her toilet was vibrating and this caused her to have a 'nervous breakdown.' She had called her lawyer in Malta, who claimed US$1,000,000 for 'loss of health and nervous breakdown'.

The Captain, together with the superintendent, had several meetings with the old lady and her solicitors and finally they accepted $12,000 in full and final settlement of her claim.

It was discovered that the cost of her cruise was $11,000, so it was obvious that all she wanted was to cover her bill for the cruise… and she achieved it.

In the after accommodation bar, the young steward was deep in conversation with a fourth engineer. They were both dark, young looking and had an air of doubt and fear about them.

'Do you think they will send some experienced, hard-boiled terrorists from the Taleban camp, or they will just send young "girls" who are full of theory and no knowledge?'

'Abdul, they told me that they will send three experienced revolutionaries: one will be a girl, and together

23

with the two of us and the two seamen already on board from Alexandria, we will be seven. If we all have experience and dedication, this should be sufficient.'

'When they come on board and we recognise them, make sure we have a meeting inside the aft locker room where the linen is kept.'

'Okay, okay. Let's split now and try not to attract attention.'

After six hours the cruise ship was ready to sail. Two hundred passengers came on board and had already found their berths and suites and already some had found their way to the bars, the amusement arcades and even the cinemas.

In the aft locker room there was a silent discussion. Every one of the terrorists knew their job and they rehearsed their roles to the minute detail. They discussed weapons, explosives and everything.

Next day at about twelve noon the beautiful cruise ship *Sea of Galilee* was in the hands of the ruthless hijackers. There was loss of life because some of the engineers offered heavy resistance, and two of them were cruelly killed by the terrorists. Also, a group of teachers from Canada, young men who were trained in self-defence and karate, tried to offer resistance, and in fact they wounded one of the Arab terrorists. Predictably, three of them were brutally butchered by the girl.

The only person who was rather passive in the whole affair was Makis, who from the beginning had been following the girl, Mary-Clare. In fact, Mary-Clare turned out to be the actual leader of the operation.

Makis could not believe that this girl, who was essentially a theoriser, could be so cruel and could so easily butcher innocent people and ordinary seamen for no reason at all, simply because they did not fit her macabre plans. She was wearing a simple T-shirt and jeans and an old black sleeveless leather jacket that was torn in several places. Makis only now noticed that her clothes were really dirty, and he should have realised from the beginning that dirty old clothes do not mean any good.

As the cruise ship was nearing Colombo, the leader of the terrorists communicated with Washington DC, London and Brussels.

'We are holding the cruise ship *Sea of Galilee* with 1,600 passengers and 800 crew. We intend to start killing thirty important passengers – VIP-types who we spotted and followed all the way until they boarded the ship – unless you agree to our two simple requests or demands:

'Firstly, you put on a proper airplane 100 prisoners you are holding at Guantanamo Base in Cuba, with sufficient fuel to reach a North African city like Algiers or Tripoli in Libya, or Cairo; and second, deposit 100,000,000 US dollars in a numbered account that we will advise you of, in Liechtenstein.

'I shall wait two hours for your answer. Exactly two hours, and listen – there will be no negotiations, no arguments!'

While this was taking place, Makis had decided to do something to avoid more killing and more disaster. He did not dare say anything to Mary-Clare because he just did not trust her anymore.

He managed late at night to get in touch with a harbour station at Trincomalee, and after a careful exchange of calls he explained to a frightened young amateur wireless operator the whole situation on board the *Sea of Galilee*. The cruise ship would be approaching the port of Colombo at about 0600 hours next morning and would wait off the port for four large tugs to help her into port. Makis told the young man that the terrorists would not allow the passengers to disembark with the excuse of a suspected yellow fever epidemic among those on board.

'Something will be done via the four tugs,' the young man told Makis. 'I will tell the harbourmaster, who is also a CIA man.'

As Makis was getting out of the linen locker, where he'd been making the call, Mary-Clare met him and pointed a gun at him.

'I cannot possibly think that you are so stupid as to communicate with anybody outside, but just in case, I am putting you under arrest and I will deal with you tomorrow.'

'You are making a big mistake. I cannot think how misguided you are!' Makis said to her angrily.

He was then tied up, both hands and legs, and he was tied to a beam in the linen store, after his mouth had been securely gagged with strong tape.

Makis thanked God that at least she did not kill him outright – which was what her explicit instructions from the 'professor' at the Taleban Camp ordained.

At midnight, there was no answer from Washington DC. The girl, together with one of the Arabs, took two young Americans who worked for the Administration in some way and duly executed them in front of the frightened passengers. This infuriated the whole community on board, including the crew and the Muslims among the passengers.

At about 0540 next morning, the engines started reducing revolutions, and after a quarter of an hour, the cruise ship practically stopped.

Makis sensed the change in the situation and tried to follow all possible variations in the rhythm of the cruise ship. He suddenly heard the noise of the approaching tugs and their sirens blowing.

There was a thud at the side of the cruise ship as if something had collided with her side.

There were two tugs on either side, and from their small holds, a dozen fully-armed, black-clad special forces troops emerged and climbed on board the cruise liner. The whole operation was very fast. It took minutes for the special commandos to be on deck. They first killed two terrorists who appeared with machine guns raised; then the commandos raced to the bridge, where they overpowered the two wild-looking Arabs who were holding their guns at the heads of the helmsman and the officers of watch.

The commandos were well trained, and it appeared that they were specially briefed for marine work because they knew the whereabouts of the accommodation and they had detailed plans of the decks, machinery, open spaces and the rooms, as well as the bars, restaurants, and even the casino and cinema.

All the terrorists, including the girl, were neutralised within a short period.

Three commandos climbed to the first class saloon, where the majority of passengers were held, but as they were trying to neutralise the two terrorist guards they did not observe that the girl, Mary-Clare, was also there, practically hidden at the bar. She turned around and killed two commandos before the third managed to throw a knife with superb skill, hitting her on the chest. She span around and fell to the ground. She was bleeding, but she was still alive when two officers of the ship lifted her up and took her away.

She was still alive when she was taken to the ship's hospital, but there, in spite of the doctors' efforts, she started losing a lot of blood. She then began shouting for a while, cursing the commandos and the fascists and reactionaries and God and the world... She spat blood all over the place, and at the very moment when she was cursing God, she took her last breath and died.

Within one hour, the *Sea of Galilee* was back to normal again, her Captain fully in charge; and the passengers were pleased that they had come through the ordeal. Of course they could not forget the shock at witnessing the brutal murder of two of their fellow passengers.

You could see several passengers circulating again in their good clothes, and some even started going to the gym and the bars. Even the cinema had some 'clients' who wanted to know what film would be showing that night.

The catering department were extremely busy cleaning the bars and restaurants, and the kitchens were again in operation. The chefs and sous-chefs were wearing their white uniforms and their white caps.

It took some time to locate Makis in the linen locker. He was very exhausted and perspiring hard. He had lost a lot of weight within the two days he had been shut inside the locker.

The Captain and officers of the cruise ship were not very sympathetic with Makis because they did not appreciate the fact that he was against the plans of the group of killer terrorists who had hijacked the ship. The old Captain in fact was extremely bitter, because this cruise would have been his last voyage before going into retirement after forty years of service as Captain.

When the Captain interviewed Makis, he changed his mind when he realised that he was the person who had communicated with the shore and given them details of the ship and the exact schedule of approach to Colombo, which enabled the anti-terrorist commandos to seize control of the cruise ship.

'What made you do that, young man?' asked the Captain.

'I do not know. I really do not understand why after years of indoctrination and training at the Taleban camp, I just felt that I could not commit murder. This could be a reason, and the other is possibly… my roots, my upbringing. You see, Captain, I come from an old established Greek family, third generation Greek-American. We are people with a tradition of shipping and so on. Could this be a reason? I do not know, but I suppose I must have some good blood in me.'

'It could be a reason. Your father or possibly your grandfather must have traditions and principles and – and I am sure they are terribly upset with your career in terrorism. They must be very, very unhappy, so listen to me: try hard from now on to change your direction, change your life.'

'What can I do, Captain? I am deeply involved in crime. My family may not forgive me. Can they forgive me, Captain? Could *you* forgive your son or your grandson if he abandoned the family and university and go to the Taleban and train for murder?'

'No, I would not forgive, young man. But your father or grandfather may be different, so try – and try hard! Anyway, I will let you disembark here, and as you were not really involved in the murder of the two passengers, I can report that you "escaped". So go, go and "repair" your life. In fact, I will not even put anything in my logbook.'

★

There was a great celebration in Washington DC that evening.

It was a party for the young given by Peter, the son of Senator Michael Glinos, and Pallas Athina, his beautiful daughter. They had both invited their friends from university, and of course, the presence of the shipping people was prominent.

The food was terrific and the wine was the best, although most young people for some reason kept to soft drinks and the tasty fruit punch. Some of the young men, especially the university boys, were deep in romance. They were trying to impress the girls and in some parts of the lounge there was quite a lot of kissing and 'love-making'.

Towards midnight there was a late arrival. It was a distant cousin, Makis, who had disappeared for a few years and nobody knew where he had been.

The Senator had especially entreated Athina, his daughter, to give Makis a good welcome and to try to introduce him to everybody.

He explained to both his children that this young man had been completely lost; he was under the influence of a young girl, a revolutionary who would stop at nothing before committing murder. This girl had taken him to a Taleban camp and for years he had been well and truly indoctrinated.

'This young man, a sort of relation of mine, appeared last year in New York, and asked for a job in the family's shipping company. Since he started work, he showed a great aptitude for learning the business and... I personally hope we can give him a chance in society.'

'Dad, who is he really?' Athina asked her father.

'Well, his grandmother was a Glinos, and she was one of the shareholders of our shipping company. His mother, a distant cousin of mine, was a wonderful woman, she married an American guy who was a Captain in our American tanker fleet, and they had two children – Makis, and a younger boy who is still at university.

'So, Athina, make him welcome. I hear that at this famous hijacking of the cruise liner last year or the year before, although he was one of the terrorists who initially carried out the hijacking, he changed his mind and was instrumental in the failure of the event.

'Anyway, see what you can do, and ask Peter to introduce him and... of course, it is not necessary to tell everybody this boy's history.'

Athina did as she was asked and approached her cousin with a glass of punch in her hand.

'Why are you sitting on your own, Makis? Come and dance with me.'

'Well, you must be Athina,' said Makis. 'Everybody in the shipping company said that you are a beautiful girl, but specifically that you have a heart of gold.'

During their first dance, Makis gave Athina a short account of his sad story, his lucky escape and his starting work in the shipping company, in the Technical Department. He told her that he had just got a nice apartment in New York and that he would be happy to see her, if she went there.

'You know, Makis, I am partly employed by the shipping company since my father left his job as the Managing Director and went into politics. So once a month I come to New York to follow certain aspects of my father's business. And to tell you the truth, I love shipping. I suppose it is in my blood.'

'Okay, Athina. See you in New York next time you come…'

The party was still going on after 4 a.m. when suddenly Senator Michael appeared. He said something to everybody, and finally went to Makis, who at that moment was in deep conversation with two weird-looking American boys. They were pressing Makis to tell them about his time at the Taleban camps and about his involvement with terrorism and murder.

'And tell us, how many people did you kill?'

'Listen, young man,' said the Senator, intervening, 'this man went through a lot. He was trained to be a terrorist and attack the American interests – worldwide – but in the end, he realised his fault and he made retributions. He saved the lives of a lot of passengers in the cruise-ship hijack that occurred last year.' He was beginning to get angry.

'So do not try to press him. Do not try to be clever because you… you have not done anything. You haven't even done your Military Service.'

'Why should I do my Military Service? Just to be sent abroad, to Vietnam or Bosnia or Kosovo and kill innocent people?'

'I understand,' replied the Senator, and in an abrupt way he turned around and headed for the exit.

At that moment, both Peter and Athina came up to him and said, 'Do not pay any attention to that guy, Dad. He actually gatecrashed this party, and we decided to let him stay instead of creating a problem. But now, we shall politely ask them both to leave or… or we call security.'

Her smiled and said politely, 'Good night, Makis. When you are in Washington, please come to see me, and when I am at the company's office in New York, I will see you. I hear that you are in the Technical Department and you are doing well. So keep up the good work. Your grandmother – God bless her soul – will be satisfied to see you back with us, back in civilisation.'

'Thank you, sir,' Makis said.

Makis went back to work next day, and deep down there were two things that were constantly in his mind. The first was to continue his good work at the shipping company and show to everybody that he intended to change his attitude to life completely, and to show that his family ties were now terribly important to him. The second thing – which was uppermost in his mind – was the strong attraction he felt for Athina, the Senator's daughter.

He tried to analyse his feelings. Was it because she was the Senator's daughter, a high-class, very rich girl who was socially exalted, a girl who moved in the very best of circles? Or was it because she took him up that night in Washington, introduced him to everybody and made him feel important – and when those two guys tried to make him feel a nobody, a dangerous terrorist, she turned the conversation around and attacked the 'accusers' so violently that they had nothing to answer?

What was it? It could not be love, or was it? Love usually comes after a period of knowing the other person, appreciating their good and bad points and usually, he supposed, usually love comes to them with physical attraction and satisfying lovemaking. Is love a final result of self-sacrifice, of wanting to do things for the person you love? Makis surely did not know. It was some sort of chemistry, physical and mental.

Somebody a few years ago had said to him that 'love meant sharing each other's pain'. At the time he did not understand the meaning of this, something an old professor of his told him.

He knew that he'd never been in love. He was too young at High School, and then he got involved with Mary-Clare. She completely devoured him and fully overpowered him. She gave him theory, all the well-known jargon of cheap communism and terrorist ideology. It was so overwhelming that he did not know how to reason. But he knew deep down that it was not love, although she had taught him the high science of lovemaking in all its glory.

One day as he was getting ready to go to Baltimore to attend one of their ships at Bethlehem dry dock, Makis realised that Washington was not far from Baltimore.

Would Athina like to go out with him, to a theatre or for dinner? He hesitated. No, he thought. Why would she? She knows such a lot of young men, she has such a wide circle of important, interesting men who would give their right arm to take her out.

Why should she be interested in going out with a man who had nothing to show for himself except a completely negative attitude towards his country, his family and society – a man who was ready to do terrorist acts, kill innocent people and... it was only an that accident he realised on the spur of the moment how wrong he was, and what a serious crime he was going to commit.

Makis was approaching the terminal to get into one of the shuttle planes for Baltimore when he realised that he had twenty minutes to spare.

He went on an impulse to a public telephone and rang Athina at her home. It was eight o'clock in the morning. A serious sounding man answered the phone and asked him to wait a minute for Miss Athina. She came and she was immediately polite and warm.

'Where are you, Makis? What took you so long to phone me?'

'I did not think… I thought that… you are so busy in Washington. I thought, you know…?'

'Stop talking in monosyllables. When will you be in Baltimore and how long will you be staying there?'

'How do you know I am going to Baltimore?'

'I have Greek blood in me too, young man. Where you are working in the Technical Department there are two secretaries who are my friends and my spies and… and they tell me exactly what you do, how your performance is going, and of course whether you have any serious attachments to any female!'

'I see. It is not fair, Athina! It simply is not fair.'

'Who says it is not fair? Life is not fair, and if you're interested in achieving something, you have to go all the way for it. Anyway, why should I give you lessons in being brave and making decisions? You did not have me when you were off in Colombo on the *Sea of Galilee*, where you decided to change your life completely – and I mean completely!'

'The money I put into the phone is finishing fast. Can we meet in Washington one evening?'

'Yes, we will, but after work hours. Do not spoil your usual…'

'I will call you tonight or at the latest tomorrow. See you soon, Athina.'

'Yes, do not leave it—' But the call was interrupted by the usual *beep, beep.*

What did Athina want to say at the end? Do not leave it too long? Do not leave your ship? Anyway, Makis was floating on a sea of happiness.

He could not believe his luck.

That night, only a few minutes after he got into his hotel room in Baltimore, there was a heavy knock on his door. When he opened it, there were two men showing him a piece of paper. They introduced themselves as FBI agents, showed him their credentials and told him that he was under arrest, the accusation being 'for being part of a terrorist group who were instrumental in the hijacking of a passenger liner and were also instrumental to the brutal murder of two innocent people'.

He was allowed to make two phone calls, one to the Senator Michael Glinos, who was reassuring and told Makis that next day he would be released. The other call was to his boss at the shipping company, just to tell him what happened and to ask him to send another member of the technical team to attend the ship in Bethlehem Dockyard.

The ship in Baltimore dockyard needed some steel renewal repairs, and they had to be done quickly because after exactly fifteen days, the ship had to be delivered for a very lucrative charter for two years. They could not afford to miss the charter, and supervising the repairs was very important. They had to put all the pressure possible on the repairers to finish the work in time.

Now that Makis could not be available, it was absolutely essential to have another engineer in Baltimore to do his job.

Next day at ten-thirty Makis had to appear in front of a judge. The Senator had dispatched one of his top attorneys, and Athina was there too.

A sworn deposition was given by his attorney, who gave the judge the facts that Makis was a member of the terrorist group under the complete influence of a certain girl, but he was reluctant in following them and at the end of the day, he was the man who gave the information to the port authorities in Colombo that resulted in the capture of the terrorist group and the saving of a lot of lives.

As regards the killing of the two passengers, the accused was in a different part of the ship and it had been proven and accepted at the time by the full investigation carried out by the owners of the cruise ship, together with the port authorities, that Makis, the accused, was not involved in the killing, and in fact this brutal murder of the two passengers was the thing that triggered inside him the resolve to cut himself off from the terrorist group; and more important, the accused managed, by endangering his life, to communicate with the authorities with the well-known results.

Athina had with her the full report and the investigation that took place at the time. She gave evidence herself, and Makis was astonished at the passion with which she related the events of the hijacking, the events leading to the attack of the shore commandos and the freeing of the *Sea of Galilee*. In conclusion, she said that the accused was now working in a shipping company. She showed he had an excellent record for over a year, and her family were prepared to vouch for him.

At the last moment, the old Captain of the cruise ship limped into the courtroom to give evidence. He was brought in by the FBI and the International Association for the Pursuit of Terrorism. He looked at Makis, touched him lightly on his shoulder and stood in the witness box. His evidence was clear, exact and passionate. At the end of his cross-examination, he raised his voice and pointed at Makis. 'This is the man who saved all these lives. He risked his life, he risked everything, and although he is not strong, and he was well and truly indoctrinated, he saved the lives of 1,800 – or rather – 2,500 people, if we reckon that the crew were in danger too.'

He stopped for a moment. He drank a little water and said to Makis, 'You remember what I told you after we left Colombo? About your life changing direction?'

Athina was so beautiful that day at the courtroom, Makis thought. She was wearing a grey suit that fitted her well and a white silk blouse. Her hair was shining and was pulled back, and in all she had the air of an aristocrat. Makis was sure that he loved her truly.

The judge, after taking into account all the evidence, and after hearing the depositions of the attorneys of the two victims of the hijacking, he ordered the release of Makis pending a report to be submitted to him, incorporating the investigation in Colombo, the investigation of the Flag State of the cruise ship, and any evidence of the political behaviour of the accused.

Makis was then in Singapore for twenty days supervising the repairs and Special Survey of their supertanker. This ship was rather old, and unfortunately, due to the latest regulations of the Classification Societies, they had to renew over 1,000 tons of steel in the internals, the main bulkheads and in the general structure.

One morning as he was inspecting a side tank with the surveyor and one of the managers of the dry dock there was a deafening explosion.

After the initial shock, they realised that the explosion came from a forward main tank, which had already been cleaned and gas-freed and steel renewals had started.

They came up and went straight to the dockyard office, where the terrible news was given to him that three workers had been killed by the explosion.

The State Police arrived within half an hour and after a few words, they told Makis that the Captain, the chief engineer of his ship and Makis himself were under arrest facing criminal charges.

It was evident that the explosion occurred because the fuel tank in question was supposed to have been cleaned and gas-freed, but this operation had not been done properly, and either the Captain of the ship or the works manager of the dockyard were in a hurry to start welding work; the result was a naked flame, an explosion and loss of life.

Over several days Makis had lengthy meetings with the lawyers of the dockyard and two American attorneys who were immediately flown from New York to represent the shipowners; there was also a representative of the P & I Club, who came from London to join their local man.

The Captain of the ship, who was under house arrest together with Makis, managed to prove to the police that during the time when the fuel tanks were being cleaned and gas-freed, there was no interference whatsoever from the Captain or the chief engineer, and in fact there was a short note from the ship to the cleaning foreman stating that the cleaning/gas-freeing should be done properly, and a chemical certificate should be produced for the Captain before any welding work or cutting could take place.

At the inquest, the judge decided to suspend the arrest of the Captain and chief engineer of the ship, and also of Makis, the superintendent; but only on a temporary basis. The order was that they would all attend the proper trial in Singapore after exactly six months when all the investigation and evidence from the workers and their management would be collected.

The night before the inquest, Athina phoned. Makis was just leaving the dockyard office when he was called on the loudspeaker. He was in constant conversation on a daily basis with the New York office, so he could not imagine who wanted him from New York at that time.

'You are having a rough time, Makis, but... I think tomorrow at the Inquest you will be finished with this rotten case.'

'How do you know about the case? It has been going on for over twenty-five days now. I am so tired, Athina.'

'I have been following this nearly every day, my love.'

'Did you say "my love", Athina?'

'Yes. What if I did? This is a free country.'

'I love you too, Athina, in fact I have loved you from the first day I set eyes on you at that party in your father's house. Athina, I'll see you in New York very, very soon.'

'Wait a minute, Makis. Do not be in a hurry. We have a long way to go, my love. A very long way to go...'

'What do you mean?'

'I will tell you what I mean when I see you next. But remember, we have a long way to go, but... but we will get there.' She paused. 'We have to clear you of your past and – and that is not easy, not easy at all.

'Then we have to get my father's approval, which is not difficult because he likes you. But still his approval is essential, especially because of the family business and the shipping business and our blood relationship.'

'By the way, Athina, when I was in New York, I asked Father Robert at the cathedral, and he said to me that the Church has no objection to such a marriage.'

'Who is talking about marriage, Makis? Do not be in such a hurry, my love.'

'Okay, goodnight, and let's talk again when I come to New York. And Athina, Athina... thank you.'

It turned out that their next meeting was not for three months, three whole months, because a few days after he arrived in New York Makis had to fly to Japan. After a few weeks there, he had to go to Rio de Janeiro to try and deliver one of their cargo ships to a Brazilian company on a three-year bareboat charter. He had no idea what a bareboat charter was, so when he was in New York he went for a whole week, every evening after office hours, to an old

Greek ex-master mariner and received lessons on the subject; and not only lessons, as he also learnt all the tricks of the profession relating to bareboat charters.

He found Rio de Janeiro an intriguing city, full of life and fun. One day, in fact, he even went to watch a football match between the local team and a famous team from São Paulo. He knew straight away that it was a big mistake to go there because he was nearly killed by the crowd. He tried to leave during half-time but it was next to impossible.

By the time he went back to his seat, the match was practically over, and he found himself pushed out all the way. This was Rio de Janeiro and Brazilian football.

When his 'turn of duty' finished he went back to New York, but when he went to the office and started to write his reports, he could not concentrate. He was thinking that he should meet Athina and 'declare his love' and discuss the 'difficulties' that she had mentioned...

At a little Italian restaurant in downtown New York, Makis and Athina were enjoying tasty spaghetti and some lovely chianti. There was a piano bar in the background and the musician was singing romantic Neapolitan songs. Athina seemed to know most of the songs and was enjoying the evening enormously.

This time Athina was very sportily dressed. She was wearing black slacks and a dark blue blouse over the slacks and a white silk scarf around her neck.

Makis was anxious to know all about her objections and the difficulties that stood in the way of their union.

'Listen, Makis. Let us play it slowly and seriously. First we must make sure that we suited to each other fully and that we are truly in love.

'If we pass this "examination" then we should try and make sure that your name is clear, that the FBI or the police have no grudge against you. And Makis, this is serious, because you remember what happened to you in Baltimore a few months ago...

'Then, we have to have the blessing of my parents. My father is a Senator and lately he has been considered for higher places in the Senate, and for the next Presidential Elections – the sky is the limit. The candidate for President is looking for a strong Vice President, and I think that Michael Glinos is this VIP.'

'Athina, it is easier to find an ordinary... very ordinary pretty girl and get married. Why should I go through the strain of getting a Senator's daughter? The answer is this: the answer is because I love her!'

During the evening they discussed a million things and they put down a detailed plan: how to act, how to go about clearing away all the obstacles for their union.

Was it really worth it? Life is so difficult and sometimes one gets disappointed with it.

Why should I look so high – that means Athina? Why couldn't I go for a lovely, ordinary Italian or Greek American girl, who could give me everything – love, sex, a family?

I suppose I must be in love with Athina, this complicated, lovely, difficult girl. So it is worth it...

By the end of the evening, they both wanted to go some place and spend the night together, but they both resisted the temptation. They parted late with a passionate, lingering kiss outside the door of the Senator's house.

'Athina, I am leaving for Mexico tomorrow. I will phone you from there and give you my telephone number and the hotel where I'll be staying, so that if you need me for something or if you have any news about what we discussed, you can get me all the time. Please call me, Athina.'

'I will call you anyway, Makis, because... because do not forget that I love you too!'

41

Three

Doomed Flight

It was bitterly cold in the small village in the North of
Finland. It was winter and the temperature was about 20°
below freezing. There was a small lake which was frozen
over, and at the end of the lake stood a small wooden hut
that was well and truly old and dilapidated. And a small
wood.

One man appeared from the side of the wood and
walked towards the hut. He approached and kicked the
door open. After a quarter of an hour there was a faint
plume of smoke from the little chimney, and from the small
window one could see a little light.

And then there was silence; silence that was interrupted
by the noise of a very small helicopter approaching from the
east. The helicopter hesitated, turned around and circled
over the little hut.

After a few minutes, from a hill to the west appeared a
skier, coming down fast. He seemed to know where he was
going. He approached the hut, took off his skis and
equipment and walked inside.

'There is one topic of conversation today, but as it is
rather important, I took the liberty of asking for a
committee meeting here.'

The blond girl in the group looked at the other three
members. The speaker drank a little tea from an old cup
and continued.

'The assassination of the leader of the terrorist
organisation is the only topic. This was decided at a full
committee meeting on the Greek island nearly two years

ago. I took the necessary precautions; I found the person who helped us in the past, who was willing to undertake the "contract". His fees were high – one million US dollars to be deposited in a numbered account in Zurich.

'It took the contact, our contact, nearly six months to find the whereabouts of the leader of the terrorists; as you know, meanwhile they committed a number of murders in suicide attacks in Israel, Lebanon, Pakistan and Ireland. They also hijacked a cruise liner, killing two Americans, and he also was instrumental in the assassination of two Members of Parliament and a Minister from Serbia.

'Our contact, after many efforts, located the leader somewhere in the north of Afghanistan, then afterwards in a camp used by the Tamil Tigers. He found out that he had a weakness for a little girl who was only fourteen and lived outside Trincomalee, and yesterday our contact was supposed to kidnap this girl and try to entice the "boyfriend" to come to liberate the little girl.'

'So what happened? Has the contract been executed? Why are you telling us all this long story?' one of the other members cut in.

'Wait, wait! You are being rude and impertinent. I am your Chairman and you have to respect my decisions.' He looked at his watch and said, 'I am expecting a call from our contact in… in exactly half an hour. In half an hour from now, our contact, if successful, will be back at his little hotel, and he will phone and report to me on the completion of our contract. He will then ask me to operate the code which would transfer one million to his account.

'When the money is deposited to his account, from our committee's account, there is a grace period of twenty-four hours during which I will have to make sure that the contract was really executed; in which case, I will have to release, properly release, the one million to him.'

'I have one question to ask the Chairman,' one of the

other members, the youngest, declared. 'Is there a way that your contact, or anybody else for that matter, could ever trace the Chairman or any one of us? This is important for all of us – and of course you too.'

'In my opinion, there is no such chance,' the Chairman said. 'We have taken all precautions; we have gone through all the misleading ways to contact the man who is doing the job; we have tried double-checking and have given him different telephone numbers which do not exist because they were subsequently cancelled through the telephone directory.'

'Okay, Mr Chairman. Let us hope that we will be immune of these operations now and for ever.'

As the Chairman was getting some more tea ready, there was a strange ring tone from a telephone. He opened his black briefcase and removed an odd-looking device which he placed on his ear.

'I am listening,' he said. He listened for about two minutes solid and then said to his caller, 'So the contract is fully complete. Then... then after twenty-four hours, after we check through our sources that the person is truly liquidated, I will release the money properly. Meanwhile, I will discuss the transfer with my committee.'

He put the gadget back in his briefcase and said, 'The contract has been fulfilled. This man abducted the little girl last night. He advised the terrorist leader at 0600 hours this morning and demanded that he personally come to bring the 100,000 dollars for the release of the little girl. At noon today, there was a meeting arranged at an out-of-town rendezvous. The terrorist was true to his promise. He appeared exactly at 1200 hours with a little pack containing the 100,000 dollars. Our man holding the little girl proceeded towards the foul-looking, bearded murderer, took the package of dollars and shot him at very close range, in the chest and the head.

'He then left the girl there and disappeared. Now we have to confirm the execution of the contract via our own ways and remit the balance – 900,000 – because as you heard, our man has already had 100,000 from the terrorist.'

He got up for a few minutes and said, 'Will you leave it to me to ensure full execution of the contract? A show of hands is sufficient.'

All three lifted their hands in approval. After a few minutes all four got up; the young man said that he would arrange for the transfer of the funds, and one after the other, at twenty-minute intervals, they went through the little door and disappeared.

After an hour, there was a small explosion in the little hut which completely destroyed it. It was as if it had not ever existed.

The Chairman was fully satisfied with his team. He managed to execute all the contracts they undertook, he managed to influence events in several countries, and they even managed to succeed in changing the political structure of certain Third World countries.

In one instance, a South American country that was flirting with extreme-left Maoist politics, was persuaded to start democratic elections and at the end, they managed to declare democratic rule.

All these, of course, were expensive exercises; but their funds were strong and they managed to replenish them with private or outside sources.

★

Senator Michael Glinos had just arrived home after a long, tiring, gruelling day. He had to face the hard-core of the Party, all the grandees and the old-fashioned 'boys' who were leaving nothing to chance in choosing their favourite man. In this case, Michael was very pleased, because at the end of the day they decided that he was the best choice for Vice President.

When he got into his study, he found his daughter there, and from the expression in her lovely face, he knew that there was something serious in the air.

'Dad, do you have time? Can I talk to you?'

'Of course you can talk to me, although I had a very, very tiring day – and evening, for that matter. Is your mother here?'

'Yes. What I have to tell you involves all of us.'

When the Senator's wife came down, Athina said, 'For the last few months, I have been involved with a boy. I mean… mean *romantically*. You both know him and although he is a distant blood relative I do not know whether you will approve of this association. The young man is Makis. Dad, you actually introduced him to me at your party, at the house-warming event we had.'

'I introduced him to you, yes, and I asked you to make him feel at home… but… but my idea was not to introduce him to you as a boyfriend or as a husband. Anyway, go on, tell us all.'

At that point, her mother intervened and said, 'Makis is a very nice and reliable boy. I heard so many good things from his boss at the shipping company. His boss told me that in the Technical Department he is the most reliable and hard-working man, and whenever there is a difficult job to tackle, especially in the repair field, Makis is the man to take it on. Also… I do not know… he gives me the impression that he has a good heart and, and I understand that through his family, he has shares in the shipping company, so he is not really poor.'

Senator Michael was deep in thought. The news his beloved daughter had just told him was a real shock to him, especially because, after the fateful events of the hijacking of the *Sea of Galilee,* his office has undertaken to investigate the matter fully, and as Makis was a distant relative who was 'lost' for a couple of years drifting around the terrorist camps, he had taken it upon himself to find out the whole truth. So he knew all that was to be known on the subject of Makis.

'Aren't you being a little hasty, Athina? We know very little about Makis himself. We know his father and mother, we know his roots, but unfortunately the young man went wrong. He went against family, Church and fatherland, and he formed a powerful association with a girl who was his undoing. I am afraid Makis has proved himself to be a weak person. If he had a little blood of his grandmother, he would not have fallen into the clutches of this girl, this murderous terrorist.'

'Dad, this is old history! Makis proved himself during the cruise. He saved the lives of so many people.'

'Athina, I reserve my right on this matter. At his moment I do not wish to give you my blessing, by any means.

'And you, Amalia,' he turned his angry face towards his wife, 'you should know better. "He has a good heart"!' he said, mimicking his wife. 'A good heart is not enough by any means! Anyway, the answer to you, my lovely daughter, is no. No – for the moment. I reserve my right for three months until I exhaust all my investigations on the subject called Makis.'

'Okay, Dad. I've said what I wanted to say. I want to add that I respect your views, I will wait to get your blessing because… because I love the guy.'

The very next day the Senator called into his private office his attorney together with a private detective who was often used by the Senate Investigating Committee on foreign nationals and drug barons.

He took a very long time in explaining to them what he

wanted. He related the time that Makis spent before the Taleban adventure and finally, he told them of the cruiser, the *Sea of Galilee*. He then gave them a 300-page judicial inquiry report on the actual cruise, the murder of the two persons, and the final events leading to the apprehension of the terrorists by the Coast Guard in Colombo.

The legal aspects of the case were discussed and at the end of the interview, the attorney asked Senator Michael, 'What is it to you? Why are you so interested in this man? I realise he is working in the shipping company that you once managed; I realise that he is a distant relation of yours, but all this is not enough. There must be one other reason!'

'Of course there is a reason, a very good reason, but... it has nothing to do with you. So start working as from tomorrow and give me a report at the end of each week. Go back to his High School days. Talk to his friends, playmates, girlfriends. Okay?'

When they disappeared the Senator placed a telephone call from his very private, red phone to a number in Pakistan.

'Is that you, Mohamet? Can I talk to you about something serious? Your fee for services rendered will be 50,000 dollars.' He then spent fifteen whole minutes relating to Mohamet what he wanted him to do, what information he needed on the subject of Makis. At the end he said, 'And I need this information yesterday, okay? Check very carefully the time he was at the Taleban camp and in Afghanistan. Did he go on any other operations or terrorist attacks?'

In the course of the next few months, the information received by the Senator on the subject of Makis was rather encouraging. Both the contacts in Pakistan and the CIA local inspectors were reporting that the young man was weak and prone to lean towards communist ideology. He seemed to feel that the materialistic world of today adopted by the American society was totally contrary to the people's ideals; however, he always felt that the terrorist organisation were completely and utterly wrong in their theoretical attitude. Makis apparently always felt that murdering innocent people and blowing up high-rise buildings or big department stores was out of his field.

A special report from North Pakistan was most interesting. It related to a meeting at the Taleban organisation when the terrorist 'professors' suggested that they hit a very famous and popular club and disco in the Island of Bali, and while all present voted for the execution of this murderous and appalling event, Makis was against the whole idea. He voted against it, and although he was only a small fry in the executive of the organisation, they finally decided to postpone the blowing up of the club and reconsider it after two or three weeks.

Of course Makis' marks in the organisation were rather low after this.

★

Makis was spending a lot of time in Singapore. He had another bulk carrier undergoing repairs, and at the same time the final Inquest for the explosion on the ship was taking place.

The technical work on the bulk carrier was easy for him; however, the legal arguments in the High Court were complex and very involved. The Captain and chief engineer had to give evidence, as did the administration of the shipyard as well as the manager of the shipyard and the boss of the repairs team.

Worst of all was that he was far away from Athina, and although there were a lot of telephone calls – especially when he was at the hotel at night – he still missed her, her companionship, her encouraging words and especially herself – her body, her sweetness, her love. Makis had no doubt whatsoever that he was well and truly in love with her.

One evening, when he was in his room after a strenuous day in the shipyard and afterwards in court, he was having a long shower when the telephone rang. It was the receptionist, who told him that a gentleman wanted to talk to him – 'a funny-looking guy,' she said to Makis. 'Sir, he insists that you come down to meet him or if you cannot, he would like to come to your room to talk to you in private.'

'Okay, okay. I will come down in half an hour and I will see him in the Oriental Bar.'

On entering the bar, Makis immediately recognised the man who wanted to see him and was very worried. He was one of the 'professors', one of the real killers at the Taleban camp, who preached and directed the cells in the murderous expeditions. This particular individual had a history of murder and successful attacks on buildings, buses and trains, and lately he'd been successful in sinking a small inland ferry boat in Malaysia.

'Hello, No.4, American boy! You see, I remember you.'

'What do you want?' asked Makis.

'I want you to come back to us. You see, nobody really escapes our organisation, especially traitors like you.'

'First of all, I am not a traitor. I have never been a traitor. If you remember, even at the camp I was always against straight-forward murder, always against killing innocent people just for the sake of demonstrating "the power of the people". You don't have to kill innocent people, women and children, in order to tell people that you exist.'

'Never mind all these excuses. The organisation feels that you had a hand in the failure of the hijacking of the cruise ship. They are not sure completely. If they were, you would be dead by now. I personally think you are responsible, and I have instructions to take you with me so that you can face the committee and the other professors and explain yourself.'

'I am not coming with you anywhere! This is a free country and you cannot force me to go anywhere against my will. In fact, I am leaving now, and all you can tell your collaborators is that terrorism and killing people never achieved anything!' So saying, Makis got up to go.

'Makis – No.4 – have a look at this person standing at the entrance of the bar. He is my assistant. He has a gun, and at my nod, he will kill you immediately.'

'If you look at the bar, the short guy standing next to the barman is a member of *my* organisation. He came with me from New York, and he is also armed... and he will not think twice about killing you and your man.'

The 'professor' went pale. He turned around to face the little 'barman' who gave him a huge smile and pointed to a bulge in his right side. The terrorist got up and disappeared into the lobby of the hotel.

Makis moved to the bar, approached the little guy, gave him a $20 bill and said, 'Well done. You acted natural, as if you were a proper Mafia hitman!'

'These were your instructions, sir, on the phone before you came down...'

Next day was the day of the Inquest when the judge would deliver his decision after investigating the matter for months. He had to go through thousands of pages of technical evidence as well as the testimonies of the Captain, chief engineer and chief officer of the tanker, plus evidence from the works manager, the welding foreman and of course the top management and administration of the shipyard.

'This was a difficult case,' the judge began. 'I am sure we cannot blame the ship, except in a small way, especially after reading the note the Captain sent to the works manager, stating that no flame cutting or welding works would be allowed without a proper gas-freeing of the tanks, and so on.

'However, I find that the ship or her insurance should contribute to the compensation for the three workmen to an amount of 100,000 US dollars, which I suppose will have to be paid by the P & I Club.' He paused.

'The shipyard,' he continued, 'is more to blame and from the investigation I managed to carry out, I found that they were expecting a Japanese VLCC with a lot of steel renewals, and they did not want to lose the job. So... so they were in a hurry to finish the other ship, and it is possible they did not do proper cleaning and gas-freeing. This is a reputable shipyard, so it is very difficult to find them guilty. They may not be really guilty, but I find that they twisted the format of cleaning and gas-freeing the ship's tanks.

'Therefore the shipyard will bear the major part of the compensation for the three dead workers.

'And on top of this, the shipyard will bear fully the repair cost of the damage to the tanker, as well as all the legal costs of this long case.'

The judge stopped for a while, drank a little water and announced, 'This decision can be appealed; however, I set very strict parameters for such an appeal.'

The solicitor for the shipyard, after having a short *sotto voce* meeting with his principals, got up and approached the judge.

'I am authorised by my principals to advise you, sir, that there will be no appeal.'

Makis felt fully satisfied. This was a great victory, and he felt that with his evidence he had assisted in the final result.

He had a tough, well-built ship's officer with him all the time now, as a sort of bodyguard, since the frightening experience he had in the hotel with the terrorist 'professor'.

He was really concerned, because he did not wish to have more problems, more downfalls, especially now, especially since he'd met Athina.

That night when he phoned her in New York to tell her the results of the inquiry and that he was coming back in a few days, he had the pleasure of hearing from her own mouth that she missed him, and that she would be waiting for him at the airport...

His first inclination was to get a ticket next day to go to New York. His mind lately had been fogged with his love for this lovely girl, but... but at the same time there was a clash, a clash between *love* and *duty*. His duty with the ship, with the company and with his tradition.

He thought, There will be other days and many opportunities with Athina... So, no ticket, and no rushing back to New York.

★

Senator Michael Glinos arrived home late that day. He'd had a long meeting with the grandees of the Party, where it was finally decided that he would be the candidate for Vice President in the next Presidential Elections. He also had several consultations with his advisers and detectives who were investigating the matter called 'Makis'.

He called his wife into the library, poured a stiff whiskey and said to her, 'My dear, it has been finally decided that I will be the choice of Vice President in the next Presidential Elections. So that's that.

'The other thing I wanted to tell you is that my worldwide investigation concerning Makis has revealed that he was a weak person. He joined the terrorists and went to the Taleban camps for indoctrination, and learned the science of agitation and provocation; but he was a stern believer that murder and killing innocent people was out. In fact, when he finally joined the others for the cruise-ship venture, he did not want to go and it was decided by the "elders" – or rather the terrorist bosses – that the girl had the authority to kill him, if and when she thought that he was endangering the outcome of the venture, or if she felt that he was a weak link. In fact, during the actual operation at sea, Makis was imprisoned in a linen locker on board the cruise ship, and he managed to communicate with the shore police from that position, and gave them instructions as to what they should do to free the cruise ship.

'All these should please our Athina, I think. So what do you think about this situation, my dear?'

'You know what I think, Michael. I told you a long time ago that I like the young man. He comes from a good family, he is kind and he loves Athina. And after all, I certainly do not want Athina to get involved with or marry one of these arrogant, crazy people that she met at university – people who have no regard whatsoever for family values, or for love, for that matter.

'You know, Michael, the other evening when we went to the Yacht Club with the Ambassador and his wife, and we had our son and Athina with us, I overheard a conversation between the young people. Their son, who's supposed to be an MIT graduate, was telling our Athina the different ways he could make love to her, in all sorts of chilling detail that gave me a headache. Fortunately, Athina successfully put him in his place and told him that if in future she found him in the same room or under the same roof as her, she would leave immediately and even call security.'

'Okay, okay, Amalia. Let's think about this matter over the weekend. Let us sleep on it, and next week when Athina comes for dinner, we will discuss it and see if she is of the same mind as when she first mentioned Makis to us. Let's see if she is still in love with him. And may God help her and protect her and give her his blessing.'

★

The little Cessna five-seater was flying at about 1,000 metres in a northerly direction. The weather was not good, but visibility was fair and in spite of the violent ups and downs, the three passengers were not unduly disturbed.

Suddenly the weather got worse and there were very strong lightning flashes. The pilot informed the passengers that he might have to ask for assistance at an airstrip as near as possible where they could come down and avoid any worsening situation. After a few minutes, the pilot told them that they were losing height. He was very worried because the passengers were not just anybody. The young man was a Congressman and the candidate for President of the USA in the next elections. He was flying to his country home with his wife and her sister.

So the pilot decided to play it safe and go down at the next airstrip that airport control indicated.

He was now down to 300 metres. The little aircraft was not steady at all. There were vibrations in both engines and suddenly he saw signs of fire in the starboard engine.

The pilot had very little experience of such situations. He wondered why they chosen him to take these very important people to this difficult destination…

Anyway, he tried again to straighten the little plane up. He was successful for a while but suddenly he realised that he was very, very low.

He lifted the controls with both his hands but all of a sudden the plane lost height and hit the ground with a nerve-shattering, deafening noise. And then there was nothing.

The fire engines and police cars from the small airfield nearby found a heap of scrap metal that had once been a Cessna. All on board were dead.

The report reached Washington within the hour and there was terrible confusion in the Government and in family circles. Nobody could understand the enormity of this catastrophe, and of course the consequences were grave because the young man was the candidate for presidency and… and he was so young.

It was left to Senator Michael Glinos to go and inform his mother, who was living in Cape Cod.

He was trembling violently when he rang the bell of the country house. A valet opened the door and told the Senator, 'I heard on the news but… she… madam does not know yet.'

They were interrupted by a female voice.

'Michael, welcome to our house! What brings you here, Michael?' But immediately the old lady saw the tears in Michael's eyes, she stopped, gripped a chair and sat down. 'Who is it, Michael? My son?'

When she got the whole of the bad news, the catastrophe of the situation, she suddenly appeared to be one hundred years old.

'He was your friend, Michael! You were going to make a fine team together. But God… God has his own agenda. But why me again, Michael? I lost a brother in the war and…'

Finally the old lady burst into tears, uncontrollable tears until the valet came in and together they sat her on the sofa.

Within minutes, the family doctor came and gave her an injection to calm her down.

At the funeral of the three passengers, the atmosphere was extremely sombre and there was nobody there who could keep back their tears, especially on seeing the two little children of the couple – who, no doubt, could not understand what was going on.

The whole Administration, Secretaries of State, Defence,

etc., Senators and Congressmen as well as the Governor of the State of New York, were present together with the families of both the dead couple and the sister.

Senator Michael Glinos was there with his wife, son and daughter, as well as some members of the shipping company and Makis, who wanted to be present in order to assist Athina if he could.

Finally there were a lot of foreign ambassadors and Heads of State because one of the deceased was well known to be on his way to becoming President of the USA.

The detachment of the Marines were very impressive, and at the edge of the field there was a single bugler who gave the salute, the Last Post, and when he finished there were three salvoes from the Air Force detachment.

The whole ceremony was very moving indeed, and Athina was in a state of deep emotion, especially because she knew the young man and his wife very well. She saw Makis down the line of people standing to pay their respects and she wanted very much to approach and talk to him. She needed his reassurance and his strong and kind words.

As she was deep in thought, she felt a pat on her shoulder. She turned to see Makis next to her. He said, 'Athina, this is life. This is to show you how unimportant we really are, how easily we can fall from great glory and a bright future to death and oblivion.'

She nodded. 'Makis, could you come to our house for dinner on Saturday evening? We will have the opportunity to discuss "our problem" with my parents.'

'Of course I will come. For some reason or other, I am hooked. I still do not know why I got involved with you – a difficult, complicated, beautiful, charming, loving little girl. As I told you before, I could be better off with an ordinary American or Italian-American or even a Greek girl without problems and...' But the smile on her face stopped him from saying more.

They had a terrific dinner at the Senator's mansion. In particular the dessert was so rich and fruity that Makis took a second helping.

After dinner the Senator took them to the library, which was a very comfortable room with leather armchairs and heavy teak desks.

'Well, Athina, I was always in favour of you getting involved with a nice, strong person who would love you and make you happy. This case was very difficult for two reasons. The first was the previous history, the bad side of the life of Makis, here, and on this score, I made very extensive research and inquiries. Now, without you becoming upset about it, I must tell you that the future and the happiness of my daughter is of paramount importance to me. I am clear now. I am prepared to give you my blessing, Athina, provided you are also willing to have Makis.

'Now, there is the second problem that arose only in the last few weeks. After the death of the candidate for the Presidency, the Party big shots are leaning towards me to stand for President.

'This is not yet definite, but if it becomes so, I will have to face all the Committees of the House, and of course before I am definitely chosen, there will be detailed investigations about myself, my life, my family – I repeat, my family – and of course I have to get voted in by the people!

'So, at the end of the day, in spite of my initial inclination to tell you to go ahead with your plans, I have to ask you to please wait for a few months until I get all the investigations sorted out and get this green light, if… if I get it at the end.'

Athina was anxious to get in the conversation.

'Dad, I am very, very proud of you and I am thrilled!'

At that moment Athina's mother came in the library and

said, 'Michael, why didn't you mention to me at all that they are considering pushing you as candidate for President? And I had to find our from a stranger – a real stranger – the French Ambassador's wife! This is terrific news. Does it mean that I may become the First Lady?'

'Not quite, my love. Not yet. It will take a great effort and luck and... I do not know what... for you to become a first lady. But now we face another, smaller problem. I just asked Athina to wait a few months, not too long I hope, before she makes any plans with this nice young man here.'

Makis finally spoke. 'I was hoping to be able to get married to the girl I love, but I heard some great news just now. I will wait as long as it takes, because I must declare here and now that I love your daughter and I will give my right arm to make her happy.'

'You do not have to give your right arm, young man. All you need do is erase completely your past, have some security with you for some time, and be yourself and follow the tradition of your family... and by the way, I would like to see your parents soon, so please arrange that they come to dinner in this house, would you? And tell Athina when they can come so I can make myself available.'

★

Makis was standing outside the Bice Restaurant in New York waiting for Athina. It was a rather warm night but he was feeling rather cold. He had a premonition, a funny feeling inside him. He went inside for ten minutes and then again he went out, awaiting his girl.

A black limousine pulled over and stopped for a moment; the electric windows came down and then it sped away again. Makis had the feeling that somebody was spying on him. He remembered the Senator telling him that he should get a security man or a bodyguard for a while. But he did not do anything. He thought that nobody would have any reason to harm him.

The black limousine came around again, nearer to where he was standing just outside the entrance of the restaurant. This time, the back window came down, and a sinister face appeared with a machine gun. Before Makis could utter a word, he heard a deafening burst of fire and at the same time he felt his legs giving way and blood coming out of his belly. Then he lost consciousness.

The last thing he remembered was Athina's frantic shout, 'Makis, Makis! No! Not now! Take him to a hospital, quick, quick! Call my father.'

For a few hours – or was it days? – Makis was completely out, totally unconscious. But things got better as time passed.

He started having some feeling in his hands and legs. His head was as if huge hammers were hitting it from all directions. He could not see.

After some time, he did not know after how long, he could see. He saw people around him as if in a thick fog. And then he saw his mother and Athina. He made an effort but it was too much so he sank back to darkness.

Next time he woke up it was better. He saw more clearly. His mother was still there, and after a few minutes Athina appeared holding some beautiful flowers. She held his hand and squeezed it. 'Welcome back to life, my love.'

At that moment two doctors and a nurse came in. They were wearing white robes and held a bunch of papers, medical reports, and so on.

They had a good look at him. They prodded his ribs, his belly, his head; they removed some of the bandages and after a long, long time, one of the doctors, the most senior of them, spoke.

'You were lucky, my friend. With the bullets you got, you should have been dead twice over!' He turned towards

Makis' mother and said, 'He has two broken ribs and a torn outer lung from one bullet. Then two bullets damaged his pelvis, but not in a way which could not be repaired. One arm is broken up near his shoulder and the last bullet superficially damaged his right ear.'

The doctor stopped for a while and then looked at one of the X-rays.

'It appears that the killers were not very good at shooting. They had a perfect line of fire, and still they made a mess of killing him. Anyway, I think we can patch him up; but it means a few weeks' stay in hospital and two more serious operations. One, in fact, is scheduled for early tomorrow morning.'

Athina was sitting next to the bed where Makis was strapped up all over, with tubes and drips. She was deep in thought. Just when everything was going right, when her father and mother had given them their blessing, there was this new attack on him. His life was in danger. Would his life *always* be in danger? Now she made sense of the anonymous note she'd received a week ago. The little piece of white paper said:

YOU WILL NOT LIVE LONG ENOUGH TO GO TO YOUR
WEDDING

She had thought at the time that this came from a jealous 'friend' – some twisted person who disliked her or her fiancé. But now the situation was serious. Makis was haunted by his past. Would it haunt him for ever?

Next morning Makis was in a better condition. He was able to speak a little, and after uttering some incomprehensible sounds he said to Athina, 'I know who is behind this attempt on my life. It is the "professor" at the Taleban camp, the man who tried to kidnap me when I was in Singapore.'

At this moment, Makis became incoherent and his words came with difficulty.

'Do not speak, my love,' Athina said to him. 'Try to rest. You can tell us all about it later.'

After an hour, suddenly without warning Makis said, 'It is him! He told me in Singapore that he would make it his purpose in life to liquidate me. But he will not succeed. Now that I have survived this vicious attack, I know what I will do... I will... I will...' Then his speech grew unclear again.

That night Athina mentioned to her father what Makis had said. The Senator asked a lot of questions; he even asked and wanted to find out the actual words Makis had used. He said finally, 'I will take care of this matter myself.'

Next day, late in the evening, the Senator appeared in the hospital, accompanied by a serious-looking giant of a man. After the usual questions as to the progress of Makis' condition, he sat near his bed and asked him, 'How do you know that the Taleban "professor" is behind this assassination attempt? Try to remember what he told you in Singapore.'

'When he – this beast – told me to go with him we were in the bar of the Sangrila Hotel. He then showed me a "heavy" standing at the entrance of the bar. When I showed him my "bodyguard", who was not really a bodyguard, standing behind the bar near the barman, he got excited. He became angry and said, as he was getting up to leave, "You will regret this! This is your death warrant that you have signed. I do not have to ask anybody. I do not need authority, I – I will liquidate you wherever you go. Even if you hide behind the CIA or the Americans, I will do it..." Then he ran out of the bar.'

'Okay, okay, Makis. Don't tell anybody – I mean *anybody* – about this conversation. You hear?'

It was several weeks before Makis could walk and was able to breathe properly. The doctors did remarkable work on his lung and ribs and also the arm and shoulder, which were really smashed up.

The day he was supposed to leave hospital, his room was full of people – family, friends, his mother and, of course, Athina and her mother.

The room was full of flowers and Makis was saying that it was a pity to leave them behind.

Athina finally decided to distribute them to all the other rooms where there were no flowers at all. On leaving, Makis gave the hospital a large donation, in the usual Greek/American style.

But still he was afraid. Afraid for his life, his future. He did not know what to do. Maybe God would help.

But still he decided to fight back. He decided that the Taleban 'professor' should not be allowed to have it his own way. He should not be allowed to have the pleasure of killing him. He was convinced that he knew the man. It was a question of life and death; but he decided that he should win.

Four

The Eagle Strikes

It was a dark, cold and depressing night at the camp, one of the most fearful training camps of the terrorists, high up in the Afghanistan mountains.

Sometimes, the winter seemed more bitter than usual, and for the young man who was pacing up and down outside the command post it was an important day. He had to attend a meeting of the 'elite' in their organisation and he – the 'Eagle', as he was known – had to explain to the others why they should authorise him to undertake this difficult mission in New York.

He was confident that he would be the only one to be chosen for this difficult and very dangerous task. After all, he was the 'Eagle', and he had earned this adjective after being successful in several bombing operations over a period of three years.

Tonight he had to persuade the committee of murderers and terrorists that he, the Eagle, was the only one to be given the task of finding and eliminating the horrible, the despicable traitor who had ruined the operation of hijacking the cruise liner, and who was the cause of other damaging actions which had brought disrespect and damage to the organisation.

The meeting with the 'bosses' went on till midnight.

To the executive, the Eagle, explained in great detail the harm done by the traitor, Makis, and after talking for a solid half-hour he concluded, 'Because of all this, comrades, I want your authority, your blessing, and with the will of Allah, I will proceed to New York or any other place in the

USA or elsewhere, to liquidate this vermin, this despicable person.'

There were strong arguments against this action, especially from the financial expert, because as he said this might entail costs of at least $100,000, or even more if the Eagle decided to engage someone or to buy a contract.

After a lot of argument, it was decided that the Eagle should be given *carte blanche* and proceed to New York without delay, although the organisation in no way wished to be associated with this action.

Next day, at about five o'clock, New York time, the telephone of Senator Michael Glinos rang.

A voice spoke from far away, after identifying himself and giving a password.

'A fearless terrorist, code-named Eagle, has been authorised to eliminate your subject, Makis – the "traitor" – so take very serious precautions, because the Eagle has never failed. And do not forget the remittance to the usual account in Zürich of the usual amount, with instructions to let him know in the usual way.'

At about nine o'clock the same day, the Senator spoke to the Managing Director of the shipping lines and told him first to advise Makis that he should postpone any plans for a wedding for about three to four months; and also to start sending him to the faraway places to attend surveys, dry-docking and repairs of their ships. He did not say anything to Makis, nor to Athina, except he mentioned to his wife that any plans for a wedding should be postponed for a few months.

★

A very distinguished-looking young man booked a hotel room in an ordinary hotel in Pehham, New York. He said that he was doing his doctorate at the university and so he wanted peace and quiet and was not to be disturbed, not even for making up or changing the bed sheets and bath towels.

The concierge of the little hotel was very surprised with the movements of the young man, because he was always well dressed. He left the hotel early morning after breakfast and never returned until late evening.

'What doctorate is he talking about? I know that to get a doctorate, you should study hard real hard,' he said to the maid one day.

'You are illiterate. You do not know these things,' she replied. 'Maybe he goes to the library and he studies there.'

Another thing that did not make sense to the concierge was that when the man arrived, he had a violin or guitar case with his luggage; but there had been no sound of any sort of music since the day of his arrival.

'Maybe he plays softly so that he does not bother us or the other guests,' said the maid, who was always in the man's favour. In fact she fancied the young, foreign-looking gentleman and although she tried to start a conversation with him she never managed to get one word back from him.

After three weeks, the young man said to the manager that he was going to be away for a week or so.

★

The Eagle arrived in Rotterdam and went straight to the Atlanta Hotel. He had heard through his important contacts that the shipping company had a large tanker to be dry-docked and have some steel renewals, and that one of the company's top technical men was going to go there. Every day he used to go around from the hotel to the dry dock where the ship was lying in the hope that he would meet

Makis. He knew the recognisable funnel markings of the shipping company and was absolutely sure that one of the superintendents would soon appear. And from the description he got from his New York contacts, it was very possible that he was right.

That afternoon, the Eagle heard that a Lloyd's Register surveyor had a meeting with the superintendent of the large tanker. He was waiting in the small canteen, and when the surveyor arrived, he approached him politely and said, 'Are you waiting for the American superintendent of the tanker? Because I am waiting for him also to discuss the paint supplies of the ship.'

'Yes. I have a meeting with him in a quarter of an hour.'

After twenty minutes an elderly man came in. He put on a blue overall and went to the office of Lloyd's Register. The disappointment of the Eagle was great because he realised that the man in front of him was not Makis.

That same evening he got a flight from Amsterdam back to New York and went back to his little hotel in Pelham, with the determination to try again until he was successful in liquidating the traitor.

Every morning he was waiting for hours at a small café opposite the entrance to the offices of the shipping company. One afternoon he struck lucky. He saw Makis with two young secretaries leaving the office, and from the large briefcase he was carrying, the Eagle realised that he was off on a trip abroad.

He decided to follow him as closely as possible. He hired a special taxi and followed the limo that took Makis with the two young men all the way to the airport.

The Eagle was used to operations like this and he managed to find out that Makis was on a trip to Santos in Brazil. Of course he was well equipped with funds, and within minutes he got himself a ticket on the same flight that was leaving the airport in half an hour's time.

During the flight, the Eagle realised that he had no weapons with him, not even a penknife; but he was hoping that in Santos he could purchase everything he wanted.

On arrival he had the shock of his life, because on going through customs and immigration he was approached by two uniformed police. In a polite way they told him to follow them to a private room. There he was examined by a senior airport policeman, who had strict instructions from New York and Washington not to allow him to land in Brazil.

It appeared that the contacts of the Senator were more influential that the Eagle could have imagined. He was given some weak excuses and weaker reasons why he had contravened certain laws of Brazil that made it impossible for him to land, so after four hours he was put on another flight back to New York.

Of course, the Eagle was extremely disappointed and very angry and vowed that next time, the traitor would not have it so easy.

He decided to go back to Afghanistan, to try and form a better plan of action; but when he discussed this with the committee, they told him to wait in New York until he received new instructions.

After a week, he found out that Makis was back in New York and was scheduled to go to Hong Kong to attend to another ship. He advised the committee immediately and he was told to follow the 'victim' – the traitor – in order to carry out the task he had undertaken.

The Eagle was now optimistic. He thought that Hong Kong would be an easier target for his plan.

He prepared his visa and everything needed, and when he found out the date of Makis' trip to Hong Kong, he got his ticket and arranged to be on the same flight. On second thoughts, he considered that this was dangerous, and he booked a new flight to Hong Kong and a room at the

Regency Hotel, where Makis was going to stay.

On checking into his room in Hong Kong, the Chinese valet came to ask 'what his wishes were'. The Eagle gave him a substantial tip and asked him to inform him immediately the 'American engineers' arrived, what the room numbers were, etc.

Late in the evening, while he was watching TV and wondering how these sinful, weak, decadent, Americans lived, there was a knock on his door. The Chinese valet came in, and was full of apologies.

'Please forgive late visit,' he said. 'The American with two others just booked in and they have very expensive, important suite; only Presidents take this suite – No.101.' He got another large tip and left, of course bowing all the way to the door.

The Eagle started watching Suite No.101, and at about 10 p.m. he saw Makis, with two strong-looking bodyguards, moving towards the lift. They got out at the lobby, proceeded towards a waiting limousine and disappeared into the night.

The Eagle decided to postpone his attack for later when Makis and the bodyguards returned.

No doubt, he thought, the bodyguards would leave the suite after they felt that their boss was safe.

This happened at about two-thirty in the morning. The two bodyguards said goodnight and appeared to be going towards the lift.

The Eagle was holding his automatic and was hidden inside a linen cupboard. After five minutes he tiptoed towards the entrance of Suite 101. He knocked and heard a voice asking, 'Who is it?'

At this moment he pointed his gun and shot at the door four times in the general direction of the voice behind the door. He heard a muted groan and realised that he must have killed Makis without a doubt. The automatic had the latest type of a silencer, so there was no substantial noise.

The Eagle rushed back to his room and waited. He put on a blonde wig, changed into modern clothing and moved towards the lift. On leaving the lift and approaching Suite 101, he saw a number of people outside the door, including the hotel manager, as well as the security guard. They were talking to Makis, who seemed in excellent health. At that moment two people came out of the suite carrying a stretcher laden with a body covered in a green tarpaulin.

The Eagle realised that he'd failed again, that he must have killed one of the bodyguards. He was deeply disappointed and bitterly angry.

He decided to let go again, and return to camp in Afghanistan and have another attempt after a while. He knew that now that a second attempt on Makis' life had been made, he would have double security and take all the precautions necessary to make it impossible for anyone to approach him, let alone kill him. The Eagle was extremely disappointed but he did not want to accept failure. The Eagle never, ever accepted failure.

On his way to the camp, the Eagle had second thoughts. Why not try a bomb in the traitor's car? This worked in many cases; it was used extensively by the terrorist group the '17th November', so why not in New York?

He rearranged his ticket, and the next day he was on his way to New York. He was met at the airport by two operations personnel who had travelled from Chicago to meet him and help him with whatever he had in mind.

They booked into a small, downtown hotel not far from the office where Makis worked and they started making plans.

Makis had arrived in New York the same day and of course the talk in the office was of the assassination of his friend and bodyguard. And Athina was worried.

'I do not like the situation at all, my love. Not at all. I am afraid, afraid for your life... Somebody's got it in his head to kill you, and we know who it is.'

They were sitting in a small Greek restaurant in Greenwich Village and they were feeling very happy; happy because they had not seen each other for a long time, because Makis was always on the move, and Athina was also busy with her work at the shipping company, and with her advanced studies at the university. However, everything – even when they had made plans to meet in a restaurant or in a hotel – had to be approved and planned by the man whom the Senator had appointed to oversee and supervise Makis' movements and protect his life.

'Athina, my sweet girl,' said Makis, 'one of these days all will be finished, and we shall be together because simply... we love each other.' He paused and went on, 'You remember the Apostle Paul's definition of love? "Love believes all, love supports all, love is hope, love never dies..."'

'Okay, okay,' Athina retorted. 'I know your love for love, and I agree with you, but if something happens to you... if something comes, then what shall I do with love?'

'Anyway, forget the dark thoughts and enjoy your calamari and the taramasalata! Nothing is going to happen to me or to you" Makis was saying these words, but he was not at all sure as he spoke.

And while the two lovers were to some extent enjoying themselves, the Eagle and his assistants were preparing a bomb to be placed under Makis' car at the shipping company's car park downtown.

Next morning, they approached the car park carefully wearing uniforms marked 'CHEMICAL CLEAN'. They passed the car, went back and one of the assistants dived underneath Makis' car while the Eagle was passing by. It took the terrorist about ten minutes to place the bomb mechanism, arrange the timer and get out while the Eagle was pacing up and down. Now everything was ready, and all they had to do was to wait for Makis to come down from his office, and enter his car. The mechanism was to be detonated by remote control by any of the Eagle's operators, who were watching from a nearby coffee room.

They did not have long to wait. After two hours, Makis and Athina, with two assistants, came down. It so happened that this time Athina saved his life – well and truly saved his life – because as the bodyguards got into the car, Athina called Makis to show him a piece of furniture at a nearby boutique. The terrorist, who was poised to detonate the bomb mechanism, did not see all the movements of the group. After all, he only expected one person – Makis – to get into the car, and they were four.

And there was plenty of movement, because Makis first got into the car, then the bodyguard asked him to get out in order to arrange the seats and the luggage, so there were a lot of goings-on.

Finally the two young bodyguards moved the car, and at the exit of the car park only one remained in it; the other went to call Makis and Athina.

The explosion was not very great. The fire was huge, but the explosion must have opened the car door and the driver was hurled violently onto the pavement. His clothes were on fire but he was alive – just alive.

Makis ran towards him, and with the help of Athina they took him inside the boutique. There they phoned the hospital and paramedics, and within ten minutes the poor bodyguard was in the operating theatre of the Bellevue Hospital.

The Senator was on the phone the moment Makis got home with Athina. He invited them to go down to Washington the next morning to discuss the whole situation.

★

They were sitting at the breakfast table in the Washington residence of the Senator Michael Glinos. He started by saying:

'The situation is becoming very serious, very serious indeed. The terrorists have tried several times to assassinate you; they've failed for the time being, but I am absolutely sure that soon they will succeed.

'The Bureau are worried also because some of these attempts were not in Hong Kong or Singapore, but on our doorstep, and the Bureau cannot accept that they are failing to protect an American citizen – a relation of mine – and to some extent, they are fearful for my own life; and I am supposed to be a candidate for the Presidency!'

'So what do we do?' asked Athina, who was really worried. 'What do you suggest?'

There was a long conversation between the Senator, an official from the FBI, Athina and Makis, and at the end they parted. They decided that Makis had to stop working, should change his address and in some way he had to disappear, for a while anyway.

The Senator finally said that he had no other option but to take the matter in his own hands and find a way to deal with the Eagle once and for all.

As they were leaving, the telephone rang. The Senator was speaking for a few minutes and at the door he told them, 'Good news from the hospital. John, the bodyguard, is out of danger. He has substantial burns to his hands and chest and his hair is all gone, however.

'He's suffering from severe shock and he has some head injuries, but the doctor thinks that he will recover, if he manages to overcome the shock and he gets out of the brain damage.'

'I am going to visit him today,' said Makis.

'You are definitely *not* going to visit him, young man! No way! You are to disappear. Do you hear this?' The Senator was abrupt and definite in his words.

For about an hour they discussed details and exactly what the Senator meant by his remark, 'You are do disappear.'

Of course the arrangements did not please Athina, and Makis didn't agree with them either, but the Senator and the FBI officer were adamant.

'No socialising, no parties, no New York or any other place for some time!'

Makis asked the FBI officer if Athina would be allowed to visit him every day. He was told in no uncertain terms that she would be allowed to visit him once a week, provided the FBI man was in agreement, and he would make all the security arrangements.

Time passed, and Makis was now living in a tiny house in upstate New York. Nobody knew the address, and nobody had his telephone number, except of course Athina and an operative of the Bureau. He was the person who from time to time went out shopping for food etc.

This was a painful experience for Athina and Makis, but there was nothing to be done!

*

At a discreet location three hours south of Casablanca on the way to Agadir, there was a small oasis with a quaint little hut. There was very little green around and only two or three palm trees.

The little hut seemed completely deserted and there was no sign of life around. Some blackbirds seemed to be floating about, but otherwise it was all deserted, with the sea in the background.

A small car appeared on the dilapidated road that passed by the hut, and as it approached it reduced speed and finally it stopped abruptly. A young, dark-skinned person holding a black briefcase got out and entered the hut. After about ten minutes there was a sign of smoke coming from the roof of the hut.

Two helicopters appeared in opposite parts of the sky and began approaching noisily, heading for the little hut. They circled around and after some effort they both touched down very near one another. One man stepped out from each of the two helicopters. The men approached the hut, and at the door they shook hands and went inside.

Out on the sea, a lovely large yacht approached the land. It was painted blue with a white stripe down the side and one could hear the noise of her powerful motors. There was no life on the decks of the beautiful yacht. One could see her fender on the top deck as well as two nice-looking jetskis. The communication equipment and radar were in full operation. She approached the deserted sandy beach, reduced speed and anchored with a lot of noise. One could see both anchors being lowered.

There was now quite a lively situation on board. One could see the Captain holding his binoculars and investigating the anchorage and the depth of the sea around his yacht.

Soon the tender was being lowered down, and with a final squeaky noise it reached the water. Its powerful motor was put in motion. A tall man, with blond hair, appeared; he spoke to the Captain for a while and went down to the tender, which left the yacht and made for the shore, driven by a dark-looking seaman.

The blond man jumped in the water and, holding his shoes, stepped on the sand. He sat down and put on his shoes; then, at a rather hurried pace, he approached the hut and entered.

'We are all here, I see,' the blond man said, 'except of course for our Member No.3, who sends his apologies. As we all know he is not well. Not well at all… but lately the doctors gave me hope that the disease has been halted and there is hope – only hope, mind you – for his recovery. Unfortunately, the strong therapy and the terrible drugs he had to take have had an effect on his legs and on his movements in general. He is now under a new drug, platinum based, which offers good prospects.

'Here today we have one subject to discuss. It is extremely important and affects our Chairman, our founder; I thought we should meet.

'As you all know the terrorist organisation and Taleban operating from Afghanistan, the organisation that we have been founded to fight, have lately decided to assassinate a young operative who once was with them. He was trained by them and ordered to organise and execute – with others, of course – the hijacking of a cruise liner.

'Apparently, the young man, who comes from a good American family with Greek roots, had second thoughts, and while the hijacking was in progress, he managed to give information to the Coast Guard in Colombo, with the result that the shore people managed to take the cruise liner over.'

'Okay, okay, chief. We know the story. Don't take so much of our time – just tell us what the problem is!' The dark-looking man, who had reached the hut first, interrupted.

'You have always been impolite and obnoxious, but… never mind. I will deal with you some other time!

'One of the terrorists, code-named "the Eagle", was on board the cruise liner, and he was the leader of that group of terrorists. He's taken it on himself to liquidate the "traitor", as they call him. He's made several attempts in Hong Kong, in Singapore and lately in New York, just outside the shipping office where the young man works. As a result of these attempts, two men are dead and one is still in hospital; but the Eagle did not manage to complete his task.

'The young man should, I suggest, be helped. He comes from a good family and he is connected in some way with a very, very influential person whom we all know and respect.

'If the Eagle manages to kill this young man, it will be a shame to our group; it will in fact mean the downfall of our organisation, as it was founded to fight against such injustices.

'Therefore, I propose that our group should give me authority to arrange, through the usual avenues, for the Eagle to be liquidated. The reason I say the Eagle only is that he has taken it as a personal insult from the "traitor", and he wants to kill him in spite of the opposition he has from his group in Afghanistan.

'This operation will probably cost us above $100,000, but I think that our funds are sufficient to secure our honour and the purpose of the foundation of our group.' Here he was interrupted.

'I do not agree that we should go – or authorise somebody to go – to the camp in Afghanistan in order to kill the Eagle. This would be dangerous and, if unsuccessful, it could have disastrous results for our group and our Chairman!' It was the dark young man again.

'I agree with you, and the proposal is that we – or rather *I* – follow the movements of the Eagle and when he is outside their camp, or the Taleban areas, I shall try to eliminate him via our usual procedures.

'I propose to put this to the vote unless you or any one of you has any questions.'

Within two to three minutes the vote was taken and the proposition was unanimously passed.

'I would like to propose to the leader that he keeps us very closely advised, because this is a difficult operation, and besides, it may take a very long time to perform,' one of the members suggested.

The leader agreed that he should keep everybody concerned advised on a monthly basis.

It was about one hour before the last member left the hut. They all disappeared the same way that they showed up. The lovely blue yacht had started her motors, after weighing up anchor, when a small explosion was heard from the hut, which completely destroyed it; and of course the inside was consumed by the fire.

★

Makis was still living some distance from New York, well away from his work. Nobody knew his address or his telephone number, except Athina and one member of the Bureau.

That evening, he was all excited because he was expecting Athina, who had to take enormous precautions to get to the little hole of an apartment he was using. He prepared a lovely meal – spaghetti and meatballs with French fries. He had bought a good French wine and a variety of fruit and vegetables.

At about 8 p.m. he saw her approaching the apartment after getting off a small bus at the end of a nearby wood.

She kissed him passionately and said, 'This is a terrible state of affairs, my love. How on earth did we manage to bring ourselves to this situation? Once, a long time ago, you said to me, "Why on earth did I have to go and fall in love with a difficult girl, rich, the daughter of a Senator? I could have chosen a nice Italian girl or a Greek girl from Astoria…" Now I can say the same thing! Why did I have to come to you, a complicated young man with a terrible past, a terrible dangerous "terrorist" that the establishment are trying to eliminate…? I could have gone to a nice, clean American boy out of Harvard Law School or an engineer or naval architect…'

'You talk too much!' Makis said.

'Any news from your father or from the Bureau?'

'The news is that the famous Eagle is in bad shape. His reputation is very low among the group of the Taleban. Now... how this news got about, I do not know. I have a feeling that we have a very important inside contact who's leaking serious information.

'I asked my father, but he declined to give me any news at all. In fact, when I pressed him a little more, he was rather indignant, upset and angry. I never saw my father to be so angry before in my life! He certainly did not want to volunteer information or say where he was getting the information from.'

They had a nice dinner and afterwards, over coffee, it was clear that they both wanted to make love to each other.

They did this with passion and great abandon, and it was past midnight when Athina remembered that somebody was supposed to pick her up, somebody from her father's group. Reluctantly she got dressed, and at the door she said to Makis, 'How long do you think this is going to last?

Makis' answer was precise. 'Not very long. Not very long at all, because people surrounding the Eagle do not approve of his moves to assassinate me, and he's lost a lot of his prestige. Also, I believe there is a move to get rid of the Eagle from our side, or from some source which I do not understand.

'You see, Athina, the terrorists are not the only ones who have the opportunities to kill people and create chaos. We are also able to fight back and defend ourselves.'

'Let's hope that one day we shall be able to be free and live a normal life,' Athina said. Then, walking quickly, she went towards the two men who were waiting for her at the end of a lake, near the thick wood.

'*Vaya con Dios!*' uttered Makis, and he disappeared inside his little apartment.

He could not sleep that night. The warmth of Athina's body was fixed in his brain like a dream, like a perfume that lingered in his room until well into the next day.

Athina too was feeling upset. She had doubts about her feelings for the first time in her young life. She was absolutely certain of her love for Makis. She was certain of her strong attraction, which was getting stronger in spite of the difficulties, the dangers and the constant threat of death.

However, lately a young American from Harvard Law School, who had joined the shipping company as a legal consultant, kept on calling her; and he never let one opportunity go by without sending her flowers and asking her out for dinner.

Only a few days ago, she had received in the mail two tickets for the première of the performance by the Kirov Ballet, together with one beautiful red rose. Of course she returned the rose and the tickets, but she had to phone the sender – Brian – and explain to him that she could not accept his invitation. She told him in no uncertain terms that she was involved with somebody else, with somebody who she cared for very much.

Brian was very persuasive and he appeared to have made very extensive investigations, as he knew a lot about her background, her education and of course the fact that she was the daughter of Senator Michael Glinos – whom most influential people in Washington reckoned as the most hopeful candidate for the Presidential Elections to come.

Athina also made discreet enquiries about Brian and she found out that he came from a good stable, his father being a well-known banker from Boston and his mother an influential person in the charity world of that city and its surroundings.

He was a handsome man, a little young for her age but 'with mature attitudes in many respects', as she heard from the shipping company.

Come on Athina, she said to herself. You cannot possibly consider anybody else other than Makis, with… with all his problems and bad past, can you?

For many days Athina was quiet, thinking only of the next time she would be allowed to see Makis.

One night when she was visiting her parents, her father said to her, 'Athina, I think that soon we may have some good news about the Eagle case. Apparently he is the only person among his group of terrorists who has this obsession with Makis, and we shall have an opportunity to deal with him in a decisive way…'

Athina could not get any more information from her father, but in some way she understood. That night Athina told her mother about the attention she was getting from Brian. Her mother, who was always worried about the 'Makis case', as she put it, was glad in a way that a nice young man was showing so much attention to her daughter; but she told her, 'Athina, you must be careful. Let your heart and brain decide. But darling, I am afraid; I am afraid in case the next time these terrorists, this Eagle, achieves what he set out to do. Take care, and let time pass.'

★

The smart young lady came out of the aeroplane and proceeded to get a taxi at the end of the line at Kabul Airport. She sat down and told the driver, 'The bird is flying.'

The driver, without uttering a word, nodded and started the engine and set off at high speed towards the town.

He had been advised long ago of the arrival of the beautiful lady and he had been given the password – 'The bird is flying'. He was not to respond to anybody unless he was told the password. In fact, two nice-looking women had approached him during the last hour, but they did not have the password.

They arrived at a small, dilapidated hotel. At the reception, the young lady presented her passport and she gave to the concierge a $100 bill.

A rather elderly man took her suitcase upstairs, going up two flights of stairs because the lift was out of order. In fact it was constantly out of order. The woman put her suitcase on the bed and opened it. She removed her clothes and hung them in the cupboard. She then removed, very carefully, some bottles of perfume and medical bottles, which she placed in the bathroom. She double checked these bottles and then removed a small leather bag containing a sort of putty.

After hiding all the bottles and 'putty' within her clothes, she went down and asked the concierge whether the restaurant was open for dinner.

She had a good dinner – rather rich – with a good wine and she was then served coffee in the nearby sitting room. The restaurant was rather empty and only two tables were occupied. She was rather surprised that the service was good and the cutlery and crockery were of such high quality.

Over coffee she started remembering the last meeting she had had with two operatives from the Bureau, who had remained completely anonymous. In fact she did not know their nationality, nor their terms of reference.

She was to go to Kabul, where there was a seminar of top executives of the Taleban and elite members of the terrorist organisation. One of these persons was a well-known operator called the Eagle. She was given a full description of this man and three photographs. In one he had a beard, in one he was beardless and one showed him wearing a Russian hat.

She had to find a way to liquidate him and return to Islamabad. There, she would have to telephone a certain number and give proof of the completion of her task. The operative words would be 'The Eagle has fallen', but... she had to provide definite proof that the Eagle 'was down', otherwise she would not be paid the $100,000.

The next morning, after dressing in a severe grey suit, she went to the Cultural Centre and asked what time the seminar was going to take place and who would be the principal speaker. The wild-looking assistant was very explicit. He told her that there would be two speakers and one was very famous, a young man who was most feared by the enemy, the man who had committed most of the sabotage over the last two years.

She asked the assistant if she could meet this famous saboteur. He looked at her Western dress suspiciously, then at her face. He then told her that 'for a pretty woman he could do anything'. Furthermore, he volunteered the information that this formidable man had taken one of the four rooms on the third floor of the Cultural Centre.

'I'd love, to meet him and congratulate him on his achievements,' she said. Then, after putting a $100 bill in the pocket of the wild-looking man, she disappeared.

After one hour, she was back at the Centre. The wild man was still there. She asked if the young terrorist, the famous man, was in his room, so that she could wish him 'everything'...

'No. They are out,' he replied, 'but they will be back after two hours.'

'Do you think you can let me look at the room of this famous man who goes by the name of the Eagle?'

'How do you know his name? This is secret. Nobody knows it!'

'Okay, okay. Nobody knows it, but I know it, because I am one of the group, and at the time of the hijacking of the cruise liner, I was with him.'

'Come with me, young lady, I will let you have a look at his room, since I see that you admire him.'

They went up together, and after taking several

precautions, he let her in and said, 'I will come back after a quarter of an hour to let you out.'

The moment the guard left, the young lady took out of her bag three bottles of liquid and the putty. She worked fast but she knew what she was doing.

She opened one of the cupboards and put one of the bottle of liquid inside, and she was manipulating the other liquids with the large lump of putty-type material. She closed the cupboard door after putting into the putty material some plastic-looking little rods.

At this moment the guard came back and said rather abruptly, 'Come on! You have to get out now, and if you tell anybody that I let you see the Eagle's room, I will kill you. I will certainly kill you!'

The smart young lady left the room, went down to the lobby of the Cultural Centre and went back to her hotel. She collected her clothes, paid her bill in cash and left the hotel, walking in the general direction of the town centre.

There, she made a short telephone call from a public call box and gave instructions about the timing of the device she had put into a particular room in the Cultural Centre.

She had to be precise in all her actions and put the chemicals in the right place, so that they would eat through the plastic and reach the Semtex. She was satisfied she had done everything correctly.

'Are you clear what you have to do? Then I will phone you after four hours – possibly from Islamabad.'

That evening the young lady was having dinner in the restaurant of her hotel in Islamabad.

She was very anxious, and in fact she was not happy about leaving the execution of this important operation to a young assistant, who, although he was well trained in the use of bombs and explosives, was only a simple operative who was paid to do a job – nothing else.

After a while she went to the ladies' room and after she made sure that there was nobody around she phoned the assistant. 'What news to report?' she asked.

'Everything went smoothly. A huge explosion, really a huge explosion, and two men were in the room. They are both dead. One of them was your friend, the Eagle. I checked with the seminar authorities, who said that the seminar was cancelled because the principal speaker had been assassinated by enemies of the people, by the materialist, capitalist animals.'

She put the phone down and went straight to the reception to clear her bill.

In her room she made a further phone call and gave somebody a bank account number.

Next morning, the lady was on her way to the airport. She was now very satisfied because her mission was satisfactorily completed, and in the course of the next two days she would be richer by $100,000. Of course, she had to share about $15,000 among several of her underworld 'friends' who had given her the whereabouts of the Eagle and arranged all her contacts in Kabul and Islamabad.

Unfortunately, she thought, half of her income went to her 'boyfriend' who was inside everything in the Arab World, in the world of terrorism, in the world of UNO and even inside the Pentagon, the FBI, etc. She started thinking whether it was a good idea to split with him now that she had entry to all the obscure 'caves' and dark places. After thinking about it she decided the answer was no. Better to have him; after all, he was a lonely, cruel person, and she loved him, didn't she?

She was sure that what she felt for him was not *love*. It was probably pity, because when she first met him at the Catholic hospital in Beirut, he was well and truly damaged, seriously wounded by an explosion at the hotel, where twenty Americans and Jewish settlers had died.

She felt sorry for him and started visiting him at the hospital. It took three months, three difficult, agonising months, for his recovery. But for reasons that she could not fathom, she persevered, and as he started getting his senses back, he started depending on her more and more. His eyes were full of sorrow and pain as he watched her taking care of him.

She took him to her little apartment when he was released from the hospital, but she realised soon enough that he was a cruel person, a person without a heart, without kindness; a person who would kill easily enough if the circumstances demanded it.

★

The special red telephone in the office of the Senator rang a few times and then stopped. At the third attempt the Senator lifted the receiver and listened to the caller. He scribbled a number and an address and said, 'Okay. It will be done,' and then hung up.

He called an executive in from the outer office, and when he appeared, the Senator asked him, 'Find out from your special friend in Kabul if the Eagle has fallen, and find out details – the time, I mean exact time – and report to me after the Committee Meeting this evening.'

When he got home late that evening, he realised that he'd had no news about the Eagle. He was angry that his executive had not reported to him what had happened. He lifted the receiver to call him, but at the precise moment the other phone rang.

'Sir, it is all done,' said his assistant. 'The Eagle has fallen at 1900 hours.' He then went on to tell the Senator exactly what happened, how it was done and all the details about the Cultural Centre in Kabul.

Later on that evening, the Senator's wife told him all about the problem of the young American lawyer who fancied Athina, and so on.

'Well, it is only natural that our Athina will attract a number of young men. But I cannot decide for her, you know that,' replied the Senator.

Well, he thought, after all the problems and difficulties we had with the Eagle! After the loss of two of our good men, and the latest effort to liquidate the Eagle in Kabul... Well, well...

Five

Trouble on the Galaxy

After a few days, Makis went back to his apartment in New York, but there was a police guard posted outside day and night. Athina was very happy and arranged to have dinner with him at their usual Greek restaurant in Greenwich Village. During coffee, Makis began saying that he would like them to arrange or fix a date for their wedding, to which Athina replied:

'I wish this too, my love, but there is a small complication.' And she told him about the attention she had been getting from Brian, the American lawyer, who in fact had phoned her father to ask that they meet the next day.

Makis appeared annoyed. 'And what about us – our love – what we've been through the last two years?'

'I know,' she replied, 'but I had to tell you all about it. I do not want to have any secrets, any shady parts in our life, in our relationship. As for me, he does not touch me in any way. My heart is given to you, Makis.'

'Yes, yes, but to tell me all about this... this American lawyer, it means that he must have touched you in some way, otherwise you would just pass this over without mentioning it to me or to anybody else.'

'I had to tell my mother, and now this person will see my father tomorrow.'

At the end of the evening, after dinner, they parted feeling slightly angry, not knowing how to weld the small crack that was created by the appearance of Brian. When they said goodnight Athina was in tears, but Makis suggested they gave it some time to make sure about their feelings for each other.

Many days went by and Athina was very unhappy. Her father told her all about Brian's visit to him and told her that he was rather aggressive and definite, in the sense that Athina's involvement with an ex-terrorist would only bring her unhappiness; and even worse, this association would not be good for the presidential aspirations of Senator Michael Glinos.

Generally, her father was not greatly impressed with Brian. However, he did tell Athina that she had to decide for herself. She knew the score with Makis, she knew that there was always a danger that the terrorists could decide to take revenge; although himself, he did not think it was probable.

Brian phoned her one evening and asked her to go with him to a grand gala evening organised by a foreign ambassador. Athina politely declined this invitation and the next evening she met Makis at their usual Greek restaurant.

For the first time since their association/love, he had brought her a gift – a lovely bracelet and necklace that he had bought from a jewellers on Madison Avenue. She loved it and wore it immediately. At the end of the evening they went to a Greek music joint, where there was nice, loud Greek music. Athina surprised everybody by dancing syrtaki and zeimbekiko with the son of the owner of the joint.

Makis was thrilled with the music, and although he was half Greek he did not know how to do these lovely dances the way Athina managed them. When they parted, again Makis did not suggest that they go to his house to finish the night.

Next day, Makis (with a bodyguard friend as usual) was on a Japan Airlines flight to Yokohama. There was a ship there undergoing damage repairs and also one of the company's new bulk carriers was doing acceptance trials.

He was booked into a lovely hotel, very Japanese looking, with lovely gardens and water jets; but its best asset was its large jacuzzi. This had strong jets of water which were supposed to give you a nice massage.

The gardens were out of this world. There were small streams of water passing under ornate bridges, and the other feature that was remarkable was the rock garden, which must have been constructed by artists.

One evening Makis was in the jacuzzi enjoying the strong jets massaging his back, when suddenly two young Japanese girls entered the room. They approached the jacuzzi area and started getting undressed. Makis thought, They dare not get totally undressed! But he was wrong, because they undressed completely, and they entered the jacuzzi where Makis was, laughing. He did not know what to do. Should he get out and expose himself, totally naked, to these laughing girls? Or wait until they finished, and then after they left he could get out and disappear... Unfortunately these girls were taking their time, so after great consideration, he stood up – completely naked – and walked towards the outer part of the jacuzzi, while the girls kept on laughing as if nothing had happened. Makis realised that this communal bathing between men and women was an old Japanese custom which had not disappeared in the present age and the modern culture of the society.

Next day, Makis was on board their brand new 75,000 ton bulk carrier that was undergoing sea trials.

It was very exciting and interesting for him. He was one of the representatives of the shipping company and they had to establish that the ship was built in accordance with the specification, and that speed and fuel consumption was as per contract.

Also, they had to make sure that the generators were working properly and that the whole electrical load could be supported when only one generator was working.

The air-conditioning units were also to be tested, as well as the fuel purifying equipment.

The ship was taken over the measured mile with half-power, three-quarters power and with service output of the engines, and every time the speed and fuel consumption had to be measured carefully.

Another problem that they had to face was the fact that the ship, and the one that came after, were three months late in delivery to the owners.

This matter was negotiated with the New York office and they had to decide there and then the exact figure of compensation which the shipyard had to pay to the owners.

Careful calculations had to be done, based on the loss that the shipowners had incurred because of her late delivery and based on freight market considerations. Finally a figure of $1.5 million was agreed, and an agreement had to be drafted by the New York lawyers who travelled especially for this reason.

Makis called Athina several times during his stay in Japan and it appeared that their relationship was improving. Makis realised that he'd been rather hard on her, because really all she had done was tell him of the existence of a man who wanted to get to know Athina with the view of... possibly... possibly marriage.

Nobody, *nobody* is going to marry Athina, he thought. But... but he realised that Athina was a great catch in the USA, and he would be lucky to have her.

Makis stayed in Yokohama nearly a month and he was glad of this break. For a very long time he had been involved with terrorists and living in fear of getting murdered. Also, he was practically a prisoner in a very small room and he was afraid, really afraid.

On his way back to New York, he stopped in Athens. Suddenly Makis thought that he would like to visit the little island where his great-grandfather came from. It would be a sort of pilgrimage, and it would give him pleasure.

But next morning when he started asking about time

schedules and so on he received a telephone call from the office in New York, telling him that he was urgently needed in Genoa, where one of their tankers was discharging cargo and there was a problem with the receivers. So his dreams and plans of visiting the little island were forgotten.

Late in the afternoon, there was another telephone call, this time from Athina. She had been expecting him to be in New York that very day and she said that she was disappointed he was not there.

He told her of his idea to visit the little island where their ancestors came from. Athina said to him, 'Do not go there on your own. Wait until we are engaged and we can both go there!'

'*Engaged, engaged?*' he shouted. 'Does this mean that the American lawyer is finished – that he is forgotten?'

'Yes, yes, Makis! You are my true love, you are my destiny!'

*

There was a lot of commotion and noise in Atlanta that week, due to the Party's convention when the candidate for the Presidential Elections in November would be chosen.

All the States had their representatives, and the hotels were absolutely full. The Convention Centre resembled a circus, only more noisy and more crowded. At least in a circus there is a dividing line between the performers – the animals etc. – on the one hand, and the spectators on the opposite side. In the Convention Centre, there was no division. All the flags and the play cards and the State signs were all mixed up and there was loud music playing all over the place.

Senator Michael Glinos was there in the hotel with his wife, his daughter and a number of people from his political environment, plus a few from the shipping company. His campaign group had done a lot of work and generally it was thought that he had more chance of being elected than the two other candidates from the Party.

The Senator was resting in his hotel room with his wife and Athina and only his immediate lieutenants from the Party machine were allowed to interrupt him at this time.

The general manager of the shipping company, who was a cousin of the Senator, was constantly with him. He kept on giving him encouraging news and said to him, 'Senator, if you fail as a Presidential Candidate, we can always use you at the shipping company! I remember you were excellent in chartering. But, but you will not fail.'

At about six o'clock the Senator left his room and with his wife, Athina and his immediate aides, he proceeded to the elevated platform, awaiting the announcement of the winner for the Presidential Candidature.

The huge room absolutely erupted in noise, shouting and music.

The police came in, together with the officials of the convention. One of them held a small piece of paper. He opened it, and all of a sudden the room was absolutely silent.

'The candidate for the Presidential Elections for this famous Party of ours is Senator Michael Glinos!'

At this, pandemonium broke out in all parts of the Convention Centre. From one corner the official band of the Atlanta Municipal Centre was playing the National Anthem, but at the same time there was such a noise that nobody could hear anything said. The Senator tried to make a short speech but nobody heard him. At the end of the speech, one could only hear '...A lot of work has to be done from now until November... Thank you all. Thank you!'

Makis heard the good news in Genoa the same night from one of the shipping executives and he phoned to speak to the Senator and congratulate him. Athina was on the phone, she was really ecstatic and very proud of her father.

Unfortunately, Makis was having big trouble with this tanker because there was some rather serious pollution from a large crack in one of the forward wing tanks, and the authorities had imprisoned the Captain and the chief engineer.

This ship had just undergone extensive hull repairs in a Singapore yard and this was her first voyage with cargo.

How can they hold the Captain, chief engineer and the owners liable for this small pollution? Makis asked himself.

The ship was in Singapore for forty days undergoing repairs, having plates and beams renewed under the constant supervision of the Classification Society. What had happened?'

Bad luck happened – that is all, Makis thought. He was absolutely sure that no judge, no proper judge, could find fault to the ownership of the ship or the Captain and chief engineer.

There was a preliminary court hearing where the Captain, chief engineer and Makis were on the one side, and the general manger and two technical directors from the shipyard were to give evidence as well as the class surveyor.

The Captain and chief engineer said that the steel work and survey work were carried out properly, all inspections by the bureau surveyors were done, and in fact there was no pressure on the part of the owners to hurry up the repairs or to cut down on any requirements and recommendations of the Classification Society. Makis made a long statement. He was cross-examined by the lawyers for the Harbour Authorities and he gave detailed statements about the number of plates renewed, regarding thickness of plates and steel sections renewed. Fortunately, Makis had with him his notebook covering the repairs of the tanker in Singapore and he managed to give precise details of the steel work and the internal work in the oil tanks.

The representatives of the shipyard added their weight to the evidence, and in spite of the representations of the yacht owners and wildlife supporters, who were shouting to high heaven, the Court decided to free the Captain and engineer. Then they set a date after six months, when the proper, full case would be heard and the evidence of the shipyard, Classification Society and ship's personnel would be fully appraised.

Makis remained in Genoa a whole week, because after the Court hearing, the ship was again allowed to continue discharge; but it took time.

Everything takes time, Makis thought, especially when you want to go back home and take care of better things than a ship's repairs!

He realised now that he missed Athina, her personality, her character and – he had to admit it – her body, her lovemaking.

After dinner he went for a walk to get away from his hotel, the Columbus Hotel. It was undergoing repairs and it was noisy and not very comfortable.

As he was walking towards the docks, he saw a large old Mercedes swerve around a woman and speed away. This woman, a rather well-dressed lady, fell to the pavement and remained there motionless. Makis approached her and realised that she was hurt, and in particular one of her arms was bleeding.

He took her to the hotel and called the hotel doctor, who gave her an injection, and gave her a proper dressing for her arm and her head, which had a rather nasty bruise. As he was leaving, he said to his patient, 'You are a lucky lady, but... do not walk around Genoa at night.'

The woman did not appear to understand the doctor, nor did she understand the encouraging words uttered by Makis.

She requested a taxi from the concierge. She bowed to

Makis, and in rather a hurry she got into the taxi and disappeared.

'She is Russian,' the concierge told Makis. 'Russian or Ukrainian or something.'

'But she appeared to be in a hurry to leave. She did not want to have a doctor or go to the hospital or anything like this,' Makis replied.

'She was definitely not a prostitute, nor easy prey, because she was well dressed; her shoes were from Milano, and she was wearing two expensive rings.'

For at least half an hour the conversation in the hotel reception went on about the accident and the nice-looking lady who had been wounded; what was she wearing, what she had said and of course her speedy disappearance.

Next morning, at about eight o'clock when Makis was getting ready to go to the repair yard to arrange for some old repair bills, there was a faint knock at his door.

Because of an old habit from the days when he was training in the mountains of Afghanistan, he asked who it was. A very polite reply came, 'I am the woman whose life you saved last night.'

This was in perfect English, without an accent. He opened the door and saw the young woman, properly dressed in day attire. She came in and stood very close to him.

'I owe you my life and I came here to say thank you. I am Russian from an aristocratic background, and I would like to give you anything you want.' And on saying this, she approached Makis even closer and her perfume reached his face and went down into his lungs.

'Would you like a coffee or tea? I think it's a bit too early for a drink, but…'

'No, no, I would like a vodka or a vodka Martini.'

On saying these last words, she leaned forward and gave Makis a lingering kiss.

Makis did not know what to make of this complete stranger who had practically given herself to him.

Okay, he thought. I've saved her life, maybe, or helped her stay alive, but why such an offer?

He tried to start a conversation about her native land and about what was she doing in Genoa. After all, Genoa is not Paris or Milan or other centres of fashion.

The woman again approached him and gave him another passionate kiss and said, 'Why don't we go to bed, and I will show you how much I appreciate the fact that you saved my life?'

At that moment Makis started getting suspicious of the whole thing. Was the accident the night before an accident or a put-up job? He said to her politely, 'Listen, my dear, I am engaged to be married and I do not particularly want to start something that I do not know how to deal with! Anyway, I am leaving for the USA tomorrow.' As he said this he moved towards the entrance of the suite, this being an indication that she should leave.

She made one more effort, saying that she had the reputation of being terrific in bed; but Makis was determined.

When the young lady left the hotel, she made a telephone call, a very short call which went something like, 'I managed nothing. The man is not as soft and undecided as you made him out to be!' She paused and then she shouted, 'So you saved fifty dollars – and I will send you the camera and the special equipment!'

On the way to New York, in the aeroplane, Makis was trying to evaluate the events of his last day in Genoa. He was almost sure that the nice-looking Russian did not just fall in love with him. She didn't decide to repay him with her favours just because he had saved her the night before. Anyway, he'd remained strong and avoided the temptation, although, he admitted to himself, there was a moment when he was not terribly averse to a wild night with the beautiful Russian...

Nobody would know. Who would know if I had a fling with the Russian beauty? I am not in love with her. I could go to New York and meet Athina and there would be no harm done.

But... but... what do I get out of a short fling with a girl like that? Nothing and... and at the same time I might get involved; this thing may be a put-up job, and while I am in bed with her, I might be photographed and then... *goodbye Athina, goodbye happiness.*

And he was in love with Athina. Of that, he was absolutely sure.

It was late when they were having their coffee on the small patio of the house in Washington belonging to Senator Michael Glinos, who was now the presidential candidate. Only the family were present: the Senator's wife, and of course Athina, and her younger brother, Peter. Makis was there too, with his mother.

Makis was in conversation with the Senator. He thanked him for all he had done to protect him against the terrorists, especially the Eagle, and most of all for the confidence he had showed in him.

Towards the end of the evening, Makis approached the Senator and his wife and said, 'Now, I wish to talk to you about a very important aspect of my life. I wish to ask for your approval and blessing to marry Athina.'

At that moment Athina approached and came close and held his hand. Makis continued.

'I know that I am not a great catch for your daughter. I know that my life was in danger during the last year or so, but you must know that I work hard in the family business, that I am now a director of the technical part of the company and most of all – *most* of all – I love Athina, I love her with all my might. She is a remarkable girl and I promise that… I will do all I can to make her happy.'

The Senator's wife appeared to be very touched with Makis' words. She turned to her husband and said, 'Michael, say something, please.'

'Makis, there was a time when I thought that you would not survive the terrorist onslaught. I was also in doubt as to your character and your strength. But now I think I know. Now I wish to give you my blessing and my wife's blessing, mainly because I know that Athina loves you deeply. So get on with the arrangements with the blessing of your parents, and God.'

Athina's mother was in tears and said, 'I suggest that the wedding be on November 5th. If Michael is elected, it will be a double celebration. If he is not elected, then at least we shall have one happy event to celebrate: the wedding of Athina.'

'That's good thinking,' Athina said. 'November 5th it is, then, if Makis agrees?'

'I agree, I agree! The sooner the better.'

The Senator was still not happy. He was afraid… afraid just in case something happened. He did not want to have any clouds on the horizon of the happiness of his only daughter. He said nothing until everybody left, but he was afraid. He decided to investigate the whole adverse and hostile organisation, with regard to Makis and himself as well. Because he too was vulnerable – especially now.

The next day Makis decided to go on a short cruise. He had owned for some time now a 48ft boat, a very reliable yacht, good for fishing, but he used it very little. His friends used to tell him, 'What is the use of having such a fine boat and having it moored in the small marina at Southampton on Long Island?' Makis agreed with his friends, but how could he use it when he was in Singapore in Yokohama or Santos or Rotterdam?

It was a fine yacht with two Caterpillar engines developing a total of 1,000HP, and this gave her a very good speed. A few months before, Makis had completely refurbished it. He had fitted a large refrigerator and ice maker, and the two large cabins were fitted with new wall material. Improved air conditioning and a large TV set were put in each cabin.

The galley was brand new, and he fitted a new microwave oven and all the latest equipment. Of course, in the navigation department, he was extravagant. A new GPS with depth sounder was fitted, as well as a new 45m radar and Laurent equipment.

His friends used to tease him about all this equipment: 'Are you going to take this boat on a tour of the world? Are you going to cross the Atlantic? Who are you taking with you? Why all this luxury in the bedrooms? We hear wedding bells...'

Makis of course did not pay any attention to the harassment of his friends in the office, but he knew that he'd overdone it a bit; yet he hoped that one day he would enjoy it.

He had a young Captain/engineer to take care of the boat. He'd been in the merchant navy before and his family lived not far from the marina.

This was a convenient arrangement for Makis, because the very few times he used the boat, all he had to do was phone Captain Jeffrey the day before, tell him what he wanted and next day the yacht would be ready in all respects.

The Captain usually brought a young Mexican lady with him, who was a good stewardess, a good cook and knew all about the care that a boat needed.

He phoned Athina in the morning and told her, 'What about going on a small cruise next weekend on my boat? We shall have a good time and we can fish, and we can swim if the weather is good.'

Athina replied, 'This is a good idea but... you never use this boat. Is it okay? Is it seaworthy?'

'It is in excellent condition and you don't need to worry about it if I am around. I know this yacht like the back of my hand.'

'Then it is okay. We go, we will swim... but as to fishing, I do not know.'

'We leave on Saturday morning, but I think it is better to drive out there on Friday evening.'

After this conversation, Makis phoned the Captain. His phone was 'not in operation', he was told by the operator.

This surprised him and he decided to call Captain Jeffrey again after two or three hours.

When he phoned again, he got the same response: the phone was not in operation.

Then he phoned his home. The Captain's wife was rather worried because, as she said, her husband had left home the day before and had not come back home at night. In fact, she thought that Makis had taken the yacht for a short cruise and they had gone to a place where the cellular phones did not work.

'Okay. Please don't worry. I will find Jeffrey and I will call you immediately.'

After phoning again in the evening, and after getting no reply, Makis started getting worried. He decided to wait until next day and if there was nothing, he thought of driving down to the marina in Southampton.

Next day, at about noon, after arranging all the pending matters in the office, he got in his car with Bob, a young port Captain in his department, and drove to Southampton.

The yacht was not there, at its usual berth, so Makis and Bob went to the Marina Authority and asked to see the man in charge.

'Your Captain came yesterday and asked for a clearance to go around the island. In fact he said that he would be away for about four or five days, so we all thought that he would be going around with you. In fact my port supervisor wanted to phone your office to see if you were there, or to find out what was the reason for the four to five days out. But I told him that we have known Captain Jeffrey and you a couple of years so we were not unduly concerned.'

'Did anybody see him leave? What time did he leave?' Makis asked.

The bosun of the marina checked his logbook and said, 'They left about 7 p.m., and in fact I was rather surprised that he left so late. Usually we do not allow departures after 8 o'clock because the shallows are rather dangerous, and at night it is unsafe to navigate in the Sound after 8 p.m.'

After making more enquiries at the marina, and after the Coast Guard was notified, Makis left with Bob to go back to New York. They were worried about the disappearance of the yacht but hoped that the Coast Guard would find the boat and notify them by next morning.

Makis remembered another old case about a small tug that had left Southampton and not returned after three days. There had been bad weather, especially in the south, but the tug was strong and could easily withstand some bad weather. She had been found floating upside down, but Makis remembered that two of the crew of four were found alive.

Next day, while he was in the office, Makis received some rather alarming news. One of the Coast Guard officers phoned and told him that the Coast Guard were monitoring the *Galaxy*, his yacht, from Montauk Point, because they thought that there were some suspicious movements going on and some unexplained actions since the Captain had left the marina at Southampton.

Furthermore, somebody had boarded the *Galaxy* in a small marina north of Southampton and got out at Montauk Point.

The Coast Guard officer then asked Makis if he knew about the movements of his Captain and his yacht, and had he known that somebody would come on board and then get out at Montauk Point?

'I had no idea whatsoever,' he answered, 'and I did not authorise the Captain to leave our berth at the marina in Southampton; and in fact, I phoned the Captain the day before yesterday, to tell him to prepare the yacht because I would come with my fiancé at the weekend to go on a small cruise, for fishing, swimming and so on.'

'Okay, sir,' the Coast Guard officer continued, 'we will watch the yacht, monitor her movements and report to you; but bear in mind that you are responsible for your yacht and your Captain, so try to find out yourself what is going on.'

Makis could not believe his ears. He had known the Captain for over two years, and before that he had served as chief officer on one of the bulk carriers of the shipping company, and generally Makis had heard from the crew that he was a good officer; although his tastes as an officer and as a person were rather expensive.

Late at night the Coast Guard phoned him and said that just a couple of hours ago a small tug had approached the *Galaxy* and a man had boarded from the tug holding a briefcase.

'We are now also following the *Galaxy* from the air and we shall board it when we think it is necessary. We shall call you again and if we think it necessary, we will ask you to come with us if and when we board your yacht.'

'I do not understand this! I simply do not understand it… I was in Washington a few days ago at the house of Senator Michael Glinos, then I came back to New York and I was in the office every hour every day. And only when I phoned the Captain the day before to prepare the *Galaxy* for next weekend to go on a cruise with my fiancée did I realise that the yacht was missing. The Captain's wife has no idea where he is, and when he is coming back. The Captain has a wife and a little daughter.'

'Okay, sir,' the officer said, 'I will talk to you very early tomorrow morning.'

Athina was very concerned about the whole situation, and when she spoke to her father, he pointed out to her that this could be a serious matter, if it was found that the Captain was engaged in unlawful actions or contraband. It then fell on the owner of the yacht to prove beyond doubt that the Captain was acting entirely on his own, and definitely without the complicity or connivance of the owner.

Next morning, the Coast Guard phoned Makis again, very early, at about 0600 hours. He said that Makis should immediately go to a small marina only ten miles from the marina where the *Galaxy* had a permanent berth.

'It appears that the Captain is heading for this little place, and the Coast Guard helicopter is following the yacht's movements, which appear to be erratic. One moment she heads east, and the next moment she changes course to south. If you think it's necessary, take an attorney with you because you may need him.'

'I do not need an attorney!' Makis shouted. 'I do not have anything to hide, personally. I will come with a friend of mine who is a Captain and works in this office.'

Makis called Captain Bob and told him to get ready. 'I will call to pick you up in half an hour. We are going to Southampton. Maybe we will board my yacht.'

In spite of the heavy morning traffic, they were at the appointed spot on time, where they met the Coast Guard officer and two seamen who worked at the Southampton Marina. They knew the Captain of the *Galaxy* and the steward/cook who often went with the yacht.

After an hour, the yacht appeared on the horizon and was approaching the little mooring place very slowly indeed. This was just a small berth that could accommodate a yacht of about sixty feet in length and five feet in draft.

It was obvious that the Captain of the *Galaxy* had no idea that he was being followed and that his movements were very closely monitored.

The boat lowered one anchor and came slowly around with her stern and tied up on the small quay. Then there was silence. The Captain went inside the saloon, and you could only hear the generator working.

Suddenly, the Coast Guard officer, with a police officer and the bosun of the marina, as well as Makis and Bob, rushed inside the *Galaxy*. They caught the Captain unawares and noticed immediately that besides the Mexican stewardess, there were two strange people talking to him.

'What is going on, Captain Jeffrey? Where have you been? Who authorised you to take the *Galaxy* away from her berth?' Makis shouted.

The Captain had no time to answer, or to utter a word before the Coast Guard officer said, 'I have authority to search this yacht and you, Captain, and your stewardess. I have a warrant and I will search the whole ship!'

The Captain shouted, 'I want my attorney to be present. I am innocent!'

'We shall see about that. If you are innocent, it will be proven. Who are these gentlemen? Are they members of your crew? Are they on board with the approval of your owners?'

'I protest most strongly. I tried to phone Mr Makis and I could not reach him. I wanted to get his authority for this… this cruise.'

Meanwhile, the Coast Guard official was searching the two cabins. He lifted the floorboards and the bilge covers and at the same time the other officer was searching the cupboards and took down the life jackets.

After one hour of extensive search, there was nothing

found. Suddenly the Coast Guard officer's phone rang. The office told him that they'd searched the man who was on the little tug and they'd found a substantial number of diamonds – some rough cut, some blue diamonds – of an approximate value of ten million dollars.

The Coast Guard director said that he was coming down to see the yacht and that nobody should be allowed to leave it before he arrived.

Captain Bob, who was following Makis' every move, then spoke to the Coast Guard officer, who was rather disappointed at not finding anything, in spite a very thorough search:

'Officer, you did not search the life jackets.'

'The life jackets? What do you expect to find in the life jackets?'

'You want to see?' Captain Bob replied. With that, he brought a sharp kitchen knife from the kitchen and started tearing apart the life jackets. The first four jackets showed nothing, but on slashing the four children's life jackets, a torrent of diamonds fell on the floor and spread all around.

'I remember a similar case in a ship off South America where all the cocaine was hidden in the life jackets and the round life-belts.'

The Coast Guard officer then said, 'You are under arrest – you, Captain, and the stewardess, also you two gentlemen.' Then he turned to Makis and Bob and said, 'You will have to remain here; you are not under arrest but we have to make sure that you were not in connivance and in complicity with your Captain.'

The policeman took Captain Jeffrey, the stewardess, and the two strangers to the local police station, while Makis and Captain Bob remained on board with as the Coast Guard officer.

Makis managed to prepare a small meal and some coffee and they all went to sleep waiting the outcome of the investigation next morning. They were also due to meet a representative of the Senator, who was coming down from Washington with the FBI officer in charge.

Next morning a senior FBI officer arrived and started the investigation with the help of Makis and Captain Bob. It appeared that the FBI were in pursuit of a gang, a high-class gang of smugglers of diamonds and uncut rubies and other precious stones. They were getting through, via helicopters and high-speed yachts, from South Africa and Namibia and then Colombia, Mexico and the USA. The distribution in the USA was a very complex operation that involved yachts, private aeroplanes and also a number of airline stewards and stewardesses.

The FBI officer declared that it was very serious for the owner of a private plane or a yacht in the event of contraband being found in their private yacht or aeroplane.

Makis could not believe his ears. He could not believe that this jinx was starting again. It couldn't be true!

First it was the terrorist organisation, then the hijacking of the cruise liner and the killing of innocent people. Then when he thought he was through, the organisation was after him; then the Eagle and the assassination attempts…

Why him? What crime had he committed?

Makis was getting angry and practically shouted at the officer, 'Just ask around about who I am, what my job is and also how many days I use this yacht. Also, the Coast Guard is well aware of my movements with this yacht. And don't be silly. Get your facts right before you throw insinuations around.'

'Yes, sir, we know all that but also… we know that you travel extensively abroad – to Singapore, Dubai, Rio and sometimes Colombia; so, we have to check. We have to eliminate you from our list of suspects and this takes time, a lot of time.'

'Sure, I understand, but do your job with some proper

priority. Check these… these guys who were moving all the contraband and see who's behind them. And leave us alone, okay?'

Later on, a senior official in the Coast Guard service arrived with some startling news. It appeared that the Captain of the *Galaxy* had been involved with a group of criminals for a very long time. The yacht was their usual vessel for stolen goods, especially diamonds and precious stones, and often the bearers used the yacht to sleep on board.

'You see, Mr Makis, you used the yacht very little, and others took up the use of such a natural place for hiding gems, and also for meetings. In fact, the *Galaxy* was a regular place – a central place – for the distribution of stones of all kinds.'

He stopped for a moment and then continued:

'This afternoon about 6 p.m., a special group of agents will come on board. They will bring a couple of divers and will go through the yacht with a fine-toothcomb.

'There will be some damage to your yacht but we are getting a technical man from the Hatteras Shipyard who will advise our men, and will also try to repair any damage for access that our agents will effect.'

After making a number of phone calls to Washington and some other obscure places, the FBI top man said, 'You and your friend, Captain Bob, are free to go home tonight, but you leave your telephone numbers with us and be available next Monday or Tuesday to attend an official enquiry in our office in Washington, where the judge will decide who will go for trial. The Captain – your Captain – as well as his stewardess, are definitely under arrest, and as you gather, their situation is very, very serious.'

The moment Makis got into his house the telephone rang. It was Athina.

'What bad luck, my love! What bad luck… it looks as if

somebody is jealous of your good fortune, jealous of your good work. I do not understand, Makis. Are we doomed to a life full of problems and troubles? Are we doomed?'

'No, Athina. We are not doomed, we are not going to accept that our love will vanish because we have these kinds of problems. We shall win at the end, provided we fight and we persevere. You see, Athina, three years ago, we've managed to go straight. We are now on a good course. We have built our love on a very strong foundation, and in spite of all these typhoons and hurricanes, we've managed to get the boat into a calm haven, and I think we shall survive. So, Athina, be optimistic, my love; we shall survive!'

They met next day in their usual Greek restaurant in Greenwich Village. They made plans about their engagement and their wedding.

They also decided to go for their engagement to Greece, and possibly go to the little island, the place where their great-grandfathers came from.

At the end of the evening, Athina said, 'Let us go to your place, Makis. I want to stay with you tonight and then I will go with you to the shipping company to see what is going on at the Public Relations department.'

They had a wonderful time all night and were absolutely and utterly in love. The telephone was put off the hook so they wouldn't be disturbed until next morning.

They had breakfast together, and Athina realised that Makis was a good, house-trained person.

'Athina, what you see is done out of love and affection for you – I'm not really a good housekeeper.'

The following Monday, the official trial and enquiry took place in Washington. The judge was very strict, and the attorney who defended Captain Jeffrey and the stewardess was an unhappy man.

Makis learned that the whole group of criminals had been discovered and there was a full-scale trial scheduled for the end of the month. Sentence would be pronounced for the Captain and stewardess at the same time as the whole group, but the FBI officer who attended the enquiry that day told Makis that he expected heavy sentences. That day Makis also learned that the divers had gone down to check the sea chests of the *Galaxy* and found about 20 lb of cocaine in a waterproof plastic container.

Special welding and cutting equipment for underwater work was brought in, and the divers removed the grids and there they discovered the cocaine – quite a large quantity of it, too!

They also found two plastic containers inside the small tender of the *Galaxy*, full of rough-cut emeralds. It appeared that the gang did not have time to separate the emeralds and the coke.

At the end of the enquiry, Makis was fully exonerated and the judge in conclusion said, 'I do not find, on the evidence that I have, any grounds for the implication of guilt for Mr Makis, the owner of the *Galaxy*. However, I find gross negligence in his recruiting of officers and crew, and if I had any doubt as to his behaviour, I would have asked for a prison sentence for him; however, he seems a very honest man and I believe the depositions of his office Managing Director as to his credentials.'

The Captain of the *Galaxy* was heavily punished. He received a three-year prison sentence and the assistant stewardess got a one-year sentence.

But it was a traumatic experience for Makis.

The *Galaxy* remained in her berth without anybody on board. However, Makis found a very good replacement Captain who had served in yachts in Miami and other Florida ports.

He went with him on the yacht and stayed for a whole day, explaining to him in detail the equipment and all the necessary machinery.

In fact, when he went back home, he called Athina and invited her to go fishing the following weekend, and she gladly accepted.

'Where am I going to sleep, Makis?' Athina asked.

'Well, there is always the deck. If you are in love, then the deck is a great luxury.'

'What about food? What are we going to eat the three days we will go out? Unless – unless you expect to catch fish and cook them in the little stove!'

'Do not worry about food. I have already made the necessary arrangements, so you will not starve. In fact, Athina, I am thinking of taking with us the Mexican girl who cleans my flat in New York. She is a good cook and she will keep the yacht spotlessly clean.'

'No. We do not want another person with us! We will lose our privacy. Anyway, my love, you told me that you can captain and navigate the yacht yourself; you can work the engines, the air-conditioning unit and all the equipment; so let us go on our own. Besides, we are not going to travel across the Atlantic Ocean. Or are you a captain of the "sweet waters", as they say in the shipping office?'

Makis made all the arrangements. He bought food, fruit, drinks, ice creams (her favourite), and he secretly went to the boat one day before the weekend to make sure that all was in good order, that the refrigerators were full, that the air conditioning was okay, that the life-saving appliances were as per regulations, and that in general the *Galaxy* was in all respects ready for them. He wanted this weekend to be an unforgettable experience.

'Are you asleep, my love?' Makis asked Athina. She was sunbathing on the foredeck of the *Galaxy*.

'You haven't moved at all for the last hour.'

'No. I was not asleep, but I was thinking. You said some

time ago that we should go to the little Greek island where our great-grandfathers came from and possibly get engaged there, or something.'

'There is no "or something". I think we should do it – make a sort of pilgrimage to the island. I believe there is a marine academy there in the name of your and my great-grandfather. Young people from all over Greece go there and they take their licence for Second Officer in the Merchant Marine.'

'But Makis, how come this little island produces such a large number of shipowners and Captains and seamen and engineers? I understand from my father that the whole population is only one thousand.'

'Well, that is an old story. I do not know the answer either, but... but you see the sea is in their blood! The young men are born practically inside the sea. Their playground is the sea. They do not have baseball and cricket and basketball, they only have the sea and the sea sports. So they become seamen, and... if they are any good they become captains or engineers, and if they are crazy they become shipowners, big shipowners!'

'But do they fail sometimes? Makis, they must go down sometimes. Do they always succeed and buy ships and become shipowners or something?'

'Of course, they do not always succeed. But they work hard. Sometimes they put all their money together – two or three brothers and cousins. They get all their money together, they buy an old ship, usually from an English company, sometimes a wreck of a ship and they all go with the ship. One is the Captain, the other is the engineer, the others are chief officers or second officers, and with hard work and a little bit of luck – you see, they need luck – they succeed. They pay the mortgage or the person who gave them the credit and... and you know the story.'

'Next year, they buy another ship and they split the

ownership and so on…' said Athina.

'Anyway, we'll go to the island next month and try to find our original roots. You never know, maybe one of the old men there will remember my grandfather or grandmother – or even your forebears.'

'What about you buying a ship? Makis, buy a ship! You know all about ships, how to operate them and how to repair them, how to maintain them.'

'You know, Athina my love, I have been thinking about this for over a year. In fact, before the problem of the contraband on my yacht, I had actually found a ship. She was rather old, a 40,000-ton bulk carrier, which a few years ago was on charter to one of our subsidiary companies. I had seen this ship when she was loading grain in New Orleans, but now I do not know her whereabouts. I remember she belonged to an old, established Greek company.'

'Makis, surely you can find out where the ship is and get a permission to inspect – what do you call it – inspect the ship's classification records? Anyway, I have some money and I am prepared to put some into this ship, provided you tell me that she is worth the risk.'

'Okay, okay, big shipowner! I will do something about it and I will tell you and soon I will get us a ship.'

It's a dream come true, he thought to himself. He was deep in thought. I have very little money, very small reserves, but if I buy an old cargo ship and get a loan from any of the banks we deal with, I can do it. The bankers know me. They may ask for references. Okay, I will get them good references from the shipping company. I can find out where most of our deposits are, which banks have them, and I may 'accidentally' tell them that I am a relative… I may accidentally tell them who Athina is. Well, well, it's a dream… but Athina likes it.

But is it possible? What about surveys? Insurances? P & I

Club? Crewing arrangements? I usually despise these engineers on board... Of course it is possible, and I will do it.

Six

A Moment of Weakness

A few weeks later, Makis and Athina were on a transatlantic flight to Rome and Athens. They went to the Hilton and had a lovely meal at the Roof Restaurant. They were joined by the Greek representative of the shipping company and discussed the general situation in Greece. It was madly boring for Athina, who wanted to know all about the little island and when or how they could get there.

The representative, who was a sympathetic old man, an old seaman, described with admiration the island and the life in the community, and of course he stated that their family and especially their great-grandfather was remembered with respect by the whole community of the island.

He also emphatically said that the majority of the young students in the Academy, on graduation, found jobs on board the ships belonging to the shipowners from the island community.

It was in the island's little church that they became engaged. Makis kept this as a surprise for Athina. He had bought the rings, and the day after they arrived, they walked up through the village. On entering the church, they were met by a priest in full robes. He guided them inside the church to the steps of the iconostasis. They knelt in front of the priest, who exchanged the rings on their fingers.

It was a moving ceremony which touched Athina's heart.

There was nobody inside the church, but when they went out there were lots of people. About twenty students of the Marine Academy had come to the church in order to meet them and declare to them how privileged they were to study at such a well-run institution – the Marine Academy which was founded by one of Makis' and Athina's ancestors.

Next morning they took the little ferry boat to the main island; but the scene at the taverna the night before was unforgettable. Practically everybody who was on the island showed up in the little taverna to offer Makis and Athina their congratulations and wishes for prosperity etc., and practically everybody brought presents – small presents and even expensive presents, such as a large solid silver icon of St Nicholas.

As they were leaving the port, they could see and admire the three little islands forming a closed, protected port. Athina was admiring the first island, the island of St Panteleimon and said, 'What a beautiful island this is! Imagine if one could build a small house there!'

'You know something, Athina, two old men last night in the small taverna told me that in the old days this island belonged to my maternal great-grandfather.'

'Then I think we should do something about it,' Athina said.

Their arrival in New York and return to the trivial tasks of the shipping company was a serious 'down' for Makis, as well as Athina.

It appeared that they were living in a different world while they were in Athens and especially on the little island. They both felt that they were practically born again.

At the weekend, Makis was invited to the Senator's house in Washington DC. He was told that it would be a formal occasion and there would be lots of dignitaries and Party officials, Senators and the Head of both the FBI and CIA.

Athina was going to pick him up at his apartment in

New York and drive them to the airport. She told him on the way that she felt that her father was worried and felt uncertain about the coming Presidential Elections on November 5th.

'Something is worrying him, Makis. Usually my father is optimistic, cheerful and a fighter.'

'Well, my love, we shall find out tonight whether there is any justification for your fears.'

After dinner, which was to all intents and purposes sumptuous, some couples left and the ladies retired to the beautiful drawing room of the Senator's residence.

Most of the men, at the request of the Senator, retired into the billiards room. There they sat down on comfortable sofas, took their brandy and started discussing the world situation.

The Senator seemed slightly anxious and suddenly he raised his voice and said, 'Gentlemen, we have a problem I wish to discuss with you. As you know I have been chosen by the Party to represent them at the next Presidential Elections. This is a great honour for me and I appreciate very much the confidence you all show in me, and of course I will do my utmost to win and in some way repay the confidence and love that the Party and the people of our country show in me.

'However, lately I have been hearing rumours; I received anonymous telephone calls, I received threats, threats to my life and my family; and these threats are not flippant threats, the sort that usually come to nothing.

'I must now take serious steps because I have a duty to the Party and to the people of our nation. But I want also your views, as to how far I can go; whether I can use the Bureau, whether I should use the police or put on to these... these people... a team of private detectives.'

'Are you not exaggerating these things, Senator?' asked the Senior House Representative.

'Before I asked you here and before I uttered one word to you, I made sure that these were real threats, and I have tape recordings – several recordings – which you can hear. I also took some photos of men snooping at the corners of my Washington office and the New York office of the shipping company that my father and grandfather founded. It is clear, gentlemen, that there are some people, some group, who want to discredit me or discredit the Party in some way.

'So I want to show you all these, and get your approval to fight back, or at least find out what it is all about.'

'We do not need to have details of all these threats, Michael,' another official said. 'We have full confidence in you and in your integrity, and I think I can speak on behalf of all of us when I tell you that you should do everything possible to protect you as a person, the Party as a whole, and to ensure the successful conduct of the coming elections.'

Makis decided it was time for him to say something.

'Senator, do you think that my past, my connections a few years ago with terrorist organisations and the Taleban, could be the reason or the motivation that your opponents might have in order to discredit you? Because if it is so, I am prepared to postpone the wedding to your daughter until after the elections.' He was really worried and spoke with emphasis.

'I do not know, but I think this is not what these opponents are driving at. I think that there is something to do with me or my family, but... but... honest to God, I cannot think what it is.'

The Senator was in a foul mood. '...Or could it be the old story – Vietnam, 1975? When I was serving in Vietnam as a junior officer in the Marines, there was an instance when we invaded a village and the three Marines who went in ahead were brutally killed by gunfire from the people living in the village. They'd posed as poor, hungry people needing food and so on. At the same time they were hiding Vietcong, who were the people who killed our advance guard of three Marines.

'The officer, my superior officer, ordered that we opened fire to protect ourselves. As a result of this incident, there were two civilians killed and two wounded. After the war, there was an investigation – a Court Martial – for my superior officer, who was somehow punished; although he was found not guilty, and the Court said that he "acted under duress, to protect his soldiers and himself".'

The Senator stopped for a while and continued. 'I was also reprimanded at the time, although I did not face a Court Martial. Is it possible that my opponents are trying to uncover old stories and publicise this incident in order to discredit me?'

'This is very weak. If they try to discredit you like this, we can throw back at them your excellent war record; Vietnam, Africa, Panama and so on. Also you hold the Congressional Medal of Honour,' a young Senator pointed out. A senior aide spoke up.

'Yes, I agree that you have full authority from us and also from the Party to investigate what is going on and take all the necessary steps to protect yourself and the Party.'

'And we think you should be tough and severe,' another operative said. 'You cannot get results by being nice and soft and polite. Crush them, Senator, like you did in Central America and Vietnam.'

On the flight back to New York, Makis told Athina in great detail what transpired and what decisions had been taken. He also told her that he suggested that their wedding should be postponed, if their association was the reason for the problems and the incidents that were thrown against her father.

'Do not decide to postpone our wedding, my love. We

have gone through hell, so I do not want anything or anybody to come and spoil our life. I will commit murder, if necessary, Makis. Do you hear me? Murder!'

'I do not particularly wish to postpone our wedding, Athina. I'd rather die than cancel the wedding. But, at the same time I owe a great deal of respect and love to your father. He helped me enormously in so many ways, and if he is in trouble now, and I can somehow help... I would do anything.' He paused. 'After all, he may be soon – very soon – the President of the United States.'

'We have to fight hard, Makis, until we achieve what we all want. And it is not easy. The other side are very powerful and rich and they will stop at nothing. I understand that the person who has undertaken to design the campaign for the opposition is ruthless and would stop at nothing.'

'Athina, I am optimistic, very optimistic, simply because in the last few years so many things have gone against us, so many things appeared to destroy us and... and in the end, everything was cleared up.'

★

It was in a thickly wooded space, deep in the Amazon, that the old couple saw signs of life. This part of the world, miles away from Iquitos, very seldom saw people. There were few visitors. The old couple had a nice wooden hut, and the little river, which was a tributary of the main Amazon river, gave a lot of life and helped the vegetation that the old man tried to develop. He was very successful in growing vegetables, fruit and all the things needed for their daily diet.

That morning everything was different. First he observed a small boat with an outboard engine buzzing up the little river towards the landing. Who would go up the river at this time of the year, the old man wondered. He followed the small boat all the way to the landing. He saw the young man get out and at a quick pace approach the dilapidated old church. It had been a church many years ago, but now one of the side walls was crumbling and one could see the interior. Only the little iron cross survived and was visible from far away.

'Come quickly!' he shouted to his wife. 'Come here and tell me what you see. Your eyesight is better than mine. What do you see?'

'Don't be so suspicious! I see a man going towards the church. What is unusual about that? They probably saw the ruins, they realised it was a church once and they stopped to see.'

'Look, look, Carmencita! There is another person approaching on a white horse. Look, look, he comes from the direction of the main road.'

As a matter of fact, they both saw a rider all dressed in black riding on a grey horse, coming quickly towards the little church. He stopped just outside the church, tied the horse to a tree and stopped as if he was talking to the horse. He stayed outside for a few minutes then patted the animal as if he was caressing it and finally he entered the dilapidated old church.

'What is going on, Carmencita? This little church has been deserted and destroyed since the end of the war. Nobody ever goes there, and a few years ago, when I was near there with Juanito, I looked inside and it was absolutely deserted and destroyed as if... as if a bomb had fallen on it.'

'Yes, old man, things change. Now we see two persons entering the church, and look, look over there, there is a motorcycle approaching – a large motorcycle – so in a few minutes there will be a third person in the church.'

'There must be something going on. Let's wait a little, let's hide behind these trees because we may see more. We may discover the truth.'

After a few minutes, there was a buzzing in the air. A small helicopter was approaching; it was a special type that could land on water. This little hydroplane came down on the river, and after a while a man got into a rubber dingy. He waited a little and another young man came down into the rubber boat. He took the oars and guided the first man towards the little landing place near the church.

A man came out of the church and went down in the direction of the landing. He shook hands with the man from the hydroplane, and after exchanging a few words they both advanced in the direction of the little church.

There was a thin line of smoke from the roof of the church as if there was someone cooking or making coffee inside.

'I think we should report this to the police when we go down to the city.'

'When are you planning to go to the city? You are not due to go there for a week or more.'

'Carmencita, what we see here are very unusual happenings and I do not understand them. It is our duty to report this to the police or somebody.'

'Okay, old man. Do what you wish.'

Inside the church, four men were sitting on broken pieces of wood and stones. There was a small table in the middle; coffee had been served in small plastic cups.

The man who'd come last on the hydroplane was speaking.

'I have called you here because we are facing rather a serious problem with the pending Presidential Elections in the States. The man who we all believe should be the next President is facing some problems, and there are threats to his life and especially to his character and his behaviour when he was in the Marines. Although we know and have investigated these matters and he is beyond reproach, the opposite side want to discredit him and ruin his chances for election, and of course they can ruin his family life.

'We were requested by important members of our worldwide organisation to make sure that the opponent of our man is stopped, and that furthermore, we ensure the election of our man at the November Presidential Elections.'

'How do we go about this one? This is a difficult question and involves a lot of people, and we are not sure of success,' one of the members interrupted.

'We are not going to canvass the fifty-one States for their votes! Oh no. We are going to discredit the opposition, after we make absolutely sure that it is him who's making these threats.

'We have found out that the opponent for the presidency has a weakness, a very strong weakness: girls, young girls... especially from a school or convent. When he was at university, he was well known for this vice. So it is possible that we hit him with this, if you approve, and if you authorise me to take this up seriously.'

'I object very much to going to such an extent. We may find it difficult with the media and our connections in the States. Also, how do we know that the person who is now a very important man with a family, will fall for the old trick of "young students from a school or a convent"? So I think that we should put this proposition to the vote.'

The vote was taken and it was two against two. The Chairman then said, 'In accordance with the by-laws of our secret society, we must ask the fifth member, our President – who as you all know is not well at all. I have his private telephone number at the Mayo Clinic and I can phone now.'

He took out his little phone, dialled, and after a few minutes a rough voice was heard.

'Sir, we are at the well-known place off the River Amazon. You know what we wanted to do and what I have suggested to the others as regards the problem off the pending Presidential Elections. Two of us are in favour of proceeding to counter the accusations against our chosen candidate by discrediting the opponent, via his old established vice with young girls, etc. However, two of our distinguished members object, so we need your guidance and your vote.'

There was silence for a whole minute, then the voice at the end of the line said, 'I greet you all. I wish I could be with you like the old days, but the good Lord wishes otherwise. I vote with the Chairman. Discredit the opponent, because he did not think twice about threatening our man, who had a reputation during the war, and he was ready to blacken his name and reputation. I think we are entitled to hit him back. God bless you, my colleagues, and see you soon.'

The line went dead. The Chairman continued and said, 'I propose that you authorise me fully to deal with this matter in my own way and I will report to you at the end, whether we have success or not. The cost will be the same as before – that is, 100,000 dollars. I propose to use the lady who helped us in Kabul with the Eagle.'

'But isn't she rather *old* to attract the opponent of the Senator? We are told he has a weakness for little girls who have just finished school or convent.'

'Yes, you are right; but this lady has a great capacity to change her appearance. She could also appear to be a Taleban warrior if she chose so. Anyway, I will study the matter and I will make sure we do not fail.'

'I propose we vote to give you authority,' the young man answered. 'Only keep us closely advised in case there are any problems.'

All four voted positive, and after this they all had another cup of coffee.

One of the members collected all the chairs and the little

table and took everything outside. He arranged them in a heap, set them alight and burnt everything.

'You see,' he said to another member, who was rather curious as to what he was doing with the fire. 'You see, we cannot blow up the old church. It would be desecration, it is a bad action to blow up a little church, although it is not a church any more.'

After twenty minutes each one of them set off on his way home or wherever they went.

Only the old man with his wife remained there and they did not know what to make of the events. They decided not to report it to the police or to the Prefecture, in case they took them to the big city for depositions and statements, which could often take months and months.

'I am sure there is something wrong going on. Four real gentlemen, well dressed came to talk. Surely they did not talk about how much is the price of soya beans, what is the value of the cruzeiro... And they came with aeroplanes.'

'Only one aeroplane came, Carmencita. Do not exaggerate things. And it was not an aeroplane. It was a hydroplane, a machine that floats on water.'

*

In upstate New York, a few days later, there was a very secret meeting between a gentleman whose name was unknown and a young lady who had just arrived from Switzerland.

The young lady was beautiful and she was impeccably dressed in a dark suit, probably by Chanel. She was silent for about twenty minutes while the foreign-looking gentleman explained to her what was expected of her and also gave her a time schedule.

At the end of his briefing she said, 'I understand everything. This is something I can do – but not by myself.

I cannot look like a sixteen-year-old convent girl any more, even with all the make-up in the world. But my niece, who is eighteen, can do it. She is a clever girl and I have used her before.

'I shall have to give her some of my fee, so it will not cost you extra. Also, I need one more week to teach her the details and the tricks of the profession.'

'No,' the gentleman said. 'We will increase the fee by $20,000 if we are successful.'

'Right. There is nothing else to say. I have a contact number for you, sir, and... and you have a contact for me.'

It was a Friday afternoon in early September. It was a fine day and the meeting was still going on. The Governor was at his best, and he had several friends and advisors to boost his ego and his views in general. All present were convinced that the Governor would make an excellent prospect at the pending Presidential Elections. He was younger than Senator Glinos, his opponent, and he was athletic and handsome and had a fine record as a Governor of the State he was serving. He had a nice family, and other than the mild drugs offences that his young daughter had been charged with during her first year at university, there was no blemish in his character or his family.

If only I could get over my little problem of falling for young girls, he thought, I'd have nothing else to fear.

During the meeting, it was disclosed that his supporters had pledged $20 million for the election campaign, so he was very pleased.

'I am going to my country home in Connecticut for the weekend,' he said to his assistant. 'You have my private numbers, just for emergency – only for an emergency, okay?'

When everybody left, he phoned his home and spoke to his wife and his younger daughter. 'I will be at the country house, honey. If you think you have some time from your charities you can come. It will only take you one hour to get there. Bring young Jill with you if she wants to come.'

'Okay, I will see how I am on Saturday morning and I will let you know.'

After an hour and a half, the Governor, accompanied only by a bodyguard, was in a shop not far from his country house. It was quite busy but of course the owner, an old friend of the Governor, left all the clients and went to attend to the needs of her 'special customer'.

The bodyguard carried some of the shopping on the way out, but the Governor also had his hands full of shopping bags and all the fruit and meat for the barbecue he was intending to hold on Sunday.

As he was stepping out of the shop, an old bicycle ridden by a young girl at high speed fell over on the pavement and collided with the Governor, who lost his grip of the packets he was carrying and nearly fell to the ground.

The girl was on the ground, and the bodyguard and a woman shopper went to lift her up. She had blood on one of her arms and her chin was all muddy and milky from the milk that came out of one of the Governor's milk cartons.

The Governor approached her and asked her if he could do anything for her – did she want to be taken to hospital? The young girl, who was wearing a school uniform, was very apologetic and she said, 'I am terribly sorry for the trouble I caused you, sir. I am okay now, it's not necessary to go to a hospital. The only worry I have is... that I spoiled my school uniform, and the Mother Superior is very strict. I do not want her to report this to my mother because I am not supposed to be in the town. I am supposed to be in class on Friday at six o'clock...'

The Governor saw a cute little sixteen-year-old in distress and his heart started beating. She is a pretty girl, nice and shapely, and she has beautiful eyes and a beautiful, well-formed bottom, he told himself.

He patted her hair a little, but by the time he turned to collect his shopping, the little girl had ridden off on her bicycle and disappeared.

What a pity, he thought. What a treasure! Well, well, maybe it's better this way. I cannot get involved in a scandal at this moment...

He thought back a few years, to when he had taken an angel of a girl to a hotel in Washington and he was caught by the boyfriend. She was only fourteen and she was a truly beautiful individual. Fortunately, the boyfriend believed him when he said that 'nothing really happened'; and with an ample bonus of $5,000, he took the tearful little girl away and thus saved the day for the Governor. It was at the beginning of his Governorship, and it was one of those lucky escapes. One thing he decided: he should be more careful in future and keep away from under-age little girls, so that he did not end up in court – or worse, in jail.

On Saturday evening, he was all by himself. He had gone fishing in the morning with the bodyguard, who was a nice guy, very well educated. They had a good time and made a good catch and they intended to cook the fish on the charcoal on Sunday at noon, when a few chosen neighbours would come round and they would all have a nice time with the barbecued sausages, steaks, potatoes, etc.

In the afternoon the bodyguard was off duty. The Governor was at the poolside reading a book when the doorbell rang. He was annoyed at the interference, but he got up and went to the door. He was very surprised to see the little girl who'd had the fall outside the store. She was wearing her school uniform and he noticed that her skirt was very short, thus showing her well-developed thighs.

She came near him and said, 'I came to apologise for yesterday. I created big trouble for you and I now realise that you are an important and famous person. I want to apologise, and if you want I will write a letter to you telling you that the whole thing was entirely my fault.'

The Governor was completely taken by surprise. 'Come in, come in,' he said. 'What is your name, little girl?'

'My name is Suzette, and I do not want my father and mother to hear what happened. The Mother Superior does not know either.'

'Never mind, Suzette. No harm done. Now come inside. Let us go to the pool. You will have a drink and tell me all about yourself, about your school and everything.' While saying this, he drew her nearer to him and pushed her towards the entrance to the pool area, and realised that she was very glad to be guided by him into the pool.

'Would you like to take a dip in the pool, sweetheart?'

'I do not have my swimming costume with me.'

'Never mind, sweetheart, you can use your panties.'

'Okay, sir, if you think so. But do not tell anybody please, or I will get into trouble.'

She took her top off, then the short skirt of her uniform, and started walking up and down beside the pool. The Governor was holding his breath and did not know what to do. The girl was so beautiful and had such a lovely, firm figure that all precautions and reserve deserted him.

'Suzette, come near me. We can have a drink, a soft drink, and we can talk.'

She same slowly up to him and gave him a kiss. He was bursting with desire but at the same time there was a sort of guilty feeling inside him.

At that moment, three photographers appeared on the walls of the pool area and it was apparent that they had been photographing the Governor from all sides. He stood up and shouted at them to go away, but when he turned back to his sun lounger, he saw the young girl all dressed up and walking quickly towards the house and the way out.

At that moment he realised that he'd had it; that he was a

victim of a clever, carefully-planned plot to discredit him.

For Christ's sake, how did they know his weakness? How did they find the little girl – the Satan – and send her to him?

It was a clever plan, horribly clever, and well executed.

What shall I do now? Now, of all times, when we have an election coming… only a few weeks away! I will find out who is at the bottom of it. And I will fight this… this… this intrusion! I have money. I have plenty of money to pay any blackmail demand that appears in the next few days!

The Governor was very upset. He was sure that this could be the end of his presidential aspirations.

But… but it could be something else. He couldn't be sure that the little girl was put up by his opponents. It could be somebody else. It could have been his wife. In fact she'd done this before, about ten years ago, when he had had this little affair with a little Mexican girl, that sweet creature from Acapulco. He remembered it all so well. He was with the Mexican girl in a hotel in Atlantic City, after he had taken her around the gaming palaces. They had a terrific time. The girl was insatiable. The only thing was that she demanded money – a lot of money – because she wanted nice dresses and a nice house for her brothers and sisters, and so on and so forth…

His wife was aware of what was going on and she hired a detective to follow him, and one day when he was in the hotel with the little girl, the detective, the photographer and the wife all appeared there.

He remembered that for months afterwards he had problems: demands for money from brothers and cousins, a lot of money. He remembered that 'this story' had cost him over $50,000; but for years afterwards he was free of problems. He pondered the present situation.

Could it be my wife again? I doubt it. I doubt it very much. Anyway, we will wait and see.

It took one whole week for the Governor to realise what was going on, and who was behind the little girl and the photographers.

His worst fears proved true, and now he realised that he needed to think very seriously about whether he should continue to try for the Presidency or stop everything.

His personal advisers were in favour of calling a meeting of the high-ranking officials of the Party and the senior politicians who had a bearing on the policy-making decisions of the Party.

The next day, while the Governor was in his office talking with his advisors and the Party officials, a small package was delivered to him, marked 'PERSONAL AND CONFIDENTIAL'. He was afraid to think what was in the package, but when everybody left, he took the decision and opened it.

It contained about twenty photographs of himself in swimming trunks by his pool at home, and the little student girl was all over him, kissing him, sitting on his knees, half-naked and of course, showing off her pronounced bottom everywhere.

There was just one simple, typewritten piece of paper with the pictures. It read:

NOT REALLY GOOD ENOUGH FOR A PRESIDENT

He decided straight away that at the meeting he'd convened for next day, of the Party elite and all the Senators and senior people, he would offer his resignation on the grounds of ill health, and say that he wanted to be near his family more.

When he arrived home that evening, his wife knew there was something seriously wrong.

'Sweetheart, something is bothering you. Something serious is bothering you!'

He held her hands and said, 'It is the old thing again. Somebody – most probably my opponents – sent a little girl last weekend on a bicycle, just outside the shop where we go shopping near our country home. The bicycle fell on me as we left the shop with Ross, the bodyguard. She seemed okay. She did not want to be taken to a hospital and she then disappeared.

'Next day, while I was at the poolside, there was a knock at the door and this girl appeared. I never thought anything sinister about her appearance. I invited her in, by the pool. Within a few minutes she undressed; she was bare-breasted and fell in the pool.'

He hesitated for a while, swallowed his whiskey on the rocks and sat down in his armchair.

'What a tragedy, my dear!' he said to his wife. 'When the girl got out of the pool,' he continued, 'she approached me, asking for a towel, and when I gave her a towel, she just embraced me and kissed me.'

He stopped again. 'Even at that moment, I did not think anything harmful of the situation, until I saw the photographers at the end of the pool, perched on the walls.'

'Oh, my dear! Not again! Not again! You are so very stupid, you are so weak!'

'What shall I do now? I cannot go on as a candidate for the Presidential Elections. I have to resign. In fact, at the meeting of the governing body of the Party I will have to declare that I am no longer a candidate.'

'No, dear. We must not be so hasty. You cannot resign now. You will destroy the Party. You will never be able to look them in the face in future. Wait until tomorrow and see their reaction.'

At the Party meeting the next day, the Governor took the chair, and after the preliminaries were dealt with, he said in a firm voice, 'Gentlemen, I have something serious to report to you. You were good enough to honour me with your votes and choose me to represent the Party and the people in the Presidential Elections in a few months' time. I will always appreciate your confidence in me.

'Unfortunately, something happened last week in my country house in Connecticut which may jeopardise our chance of winning the Presidency, and may be detrimental to the chances of the Party.'

He stopped for a while, dabbed the sweat from his forehead with his silk handkerchief, and went on to tell the elite, the Senators and the top administration of the Party exactly what had happened at the pool side of his country home.

There was dead silence in the room. After a few minutes the female Senator leading the majority in the House said, 'This is very serious. Very serious indeed, but we must stay calm. We must think. Personally, I have all confidence in the Governor, although he has let us down; he let his well-known weakness almost spoil his chances of election. But… but nobody is perfect. We must see how we can repair the damage.'

'No! I do not agree,' a young Senator interjected. 'I think we should try and find a new candidate, somebody with impeccable character, somebody without blemish. Of course the legal side of the Elections has to be followed, and the only way we can withdraw the name of our candidate is for health reasons.'

'How can we say "health reasons"? At the convention and before, we were promoting the Governor as a very young, fit and healthy man, a bull of a person with more vigour than the opposition, Senator Glinos. How can we now go to the people and say that our candidate is sick and present another candidate? We have no time to promote and build up somebody new, somebody unknown, starting from scratch!'

The meeting went on for three hours. The Governor did not say much, except that he put his fate in the hands of the committee and the Party elite.

At the end it was decided to have a full meeting of the Party in its entirety to decide what to do; meanwhile, it was to be a secret matter and nothing was to be passed to the press or the people.

Seven

Scandal

Makis was preparing for a trip to Yokohama. They had a bulk carrier in dry dock and also they had sea trials for one of their VLCC oil tankers that was being built by IHI. He had several meetings to attend within the shipping company but he wanted to 'steal' the weekend to go with Athina in the yacht and enjoy themselves.

At the same time he got into confidential negotiations to buy a ship, the *Dream Come True*.

During the weeks that went by, Athina kept on asking him whether he had made any decisions to buy a ship, and whether he'd located the old ship that he had fancied some time ago – the one he thought was a possibility as far as his finances were concerned.

He was speaking to an old, established London broker, who 'produced' for him an old 40,000-tonne bulk carrier built in Germany. She seemed a strong ship and she had good gear, 25-ton cranes, and she was fitted with a Sulzer engine. The English broker said to him that he could get it cheaper because she was due a Special Survey, and also the owner would give 70% credit at a reasonable interest rate of 6½%.

Makis made a low offer which was declined by the owner, but the owner was on holiday and promised the old broker he'd reconsider the matter on his return at the end of September.

Meanwhile, Makis checked the ship's Classification Records, which showed that over the years she had been kept in good general condition.

At the beginning of October, the owner spoke to Makis himself and told him that the ship was due to load coal in Norfolk, Virginia, and asked him to go and inspect the ship so that all that remained was to discuss price.

The inspection in Norfolk was satisfactory. Makis could not sleep the night he came back to New York, but he told nobody a thing except Captain Bob, the port Captain and his close friend.

'Could this be the *Dream Come True*? Why not?'

Athina was all for going away at the weekend. The only problem was that she wanted to invite her brother, Peter, with his new girlfriend. They were down from the university for a few days, and Athina had started liking this girl. She was from a Scandinavian background, or rather a third-generation American-Norwegian home. Her father was from Chicago and her mother from Boston, and the young lady was at the same university as Athina's brother.

Everything was arranged for them to meet on the *Galaxy* in Southampton Marina. Makis bought all the necessary food and Athina was supposed to buy vegetables and desserts. The seaman who was looking after the yacht was asked to take the necessary bunkers and water, so that by Saturday morning when Makis arrived, everything would be ready. Athina arrived soon after, and just before ten o'clock her brother arrived with the young girl, bringing a chocolate cake and all kinds of fruit.

They sailed away about noon. The weather was good and there was a wind from the north-east.

Over lunch, Athina told Makis that she had heard from her father's sources that they were very optimistic about the outcome of the elections, and that there was some sort of a serious problem with the Senator's opponent. She did not know what was going on, but there was a serious problem which the man in the Senator's group thought would have to come out in the next week or so.

'I wonder what it can be,' Makis said. 'It could be a sex scandal, because I heard some time ago – about the time of their Party Convention – that the Governor who won the nomination had once had a problem with a young Mexican girl.'

'Come on, let's go out and swim,' Peter said. 'We are in a fantastic cove and the sea is like crystal.'

'Okay,' Athina said. 'Let's go swimming and if the seaman – what is his name? – wants, he can fish around here.'

'His name is Joseph, but I do not really know his real name. I think we have found a good man, a good seaman and he is also a family man.'

'Have you followed what he does, and where he goes, my love? I am afraid lately, I am afraid about everything. So many things have happened to us that… that I am afraid. Terrorists, hijacking, assassination attempts, the Eagle – and lately diamond smuggling with the *Galaxy*. I am afraid, Makis. I want to get married to you, and live together, live in peace and have a family, if possible away from here.'

'Do not worry, I am careful now, Athina. I have to be careful. Fortunately, my training in Afghanistan with the Taleban taught me a lot of things. I promise you, I promise to God and your parents that I will protect you. I will protect you with my life and… well, I've said it all.'

Their catch that day was very good. They caught enough – about ten kilos of several kinds of fish – and in the evening they anchored again off Montauk Point and prepared the fish for frying. The sailor, Joseph, was very good at this sort of operation. Within an hour they had fried fish and barbecued ribs and they had a variety of roast potatoes.

They had a lovely dinner and then all went to sleep, rather exhausted with the fishing and swimming and talking… yes, talking. 'Sometimes talking can be a very strenuous exercise,' Athina said.

On the next day, they took it easy. They had a late breakfast, and it was nearly noon when they raised the anchor and went out into of the ocean. There were a lot of boats around, and far away, on the horizon, they could see a number of cargo ships and oil tankers.

Makis tried to explain to Athina the new idea of accepting only double-skin oil tankers to trade within the American ports.

'It is all a question of avoiding pollution, that is to say minimising pollution. You see, my love, if an oil tanker has a collision with another ship, or if she has hit the rocks, then the shell is fractured and penetrated; but there is always the inner "skin" that can remain intact and the oil will not seep into the sea.'

'Does it cost much to have double-skin tanker?'

'Well, it does. We are talking about 1.5 to 2 million dollars in steel weight etc., and also you have a certain decrease in oil-carrying capacity.' He paused. 'You see, personally, I am not convinced that having double-skin tankers is the answer to the question of avoiding pollution. I have serious doubts about the whole idea, but the US Maritime Administration have adopted the scheme, and there is nothing that can change their mind. Also, lately there was an old tanker that went aground off the Spanish coast and there was serious pollution. Finally the ship sank and thousands of tons of crude leaked out. As a result the European administrations are moving towards a decision not to allow tankers in their ports unless they too have a double-skin.'

'What is going to happen to all the hundreds of tankers – single-hull tankers – that trade in European waters?' Athina asked. 'We have a number of tankers in the company and none of them have a double skin. I understand that only the latest VLCC we are building at IHI in Japan will have double skin.'

'Well, honey, I do not know what is going to happen, but... but do not strain your lovely little head with these difficult problem; let the men and the IMO decide these things.'

'I do not agree that I should not bother with these things because I am a woman!'

'No, my love. I apologise. I do not mean because you are a woman, and especially you, cannot deal with problems like shipping, pollution etc. Anyway, your position in the company is more important and it is much higher than mine.' And after saying this, Makis went and gave Athina a long, passionate kiss.

★

On the aeroplane on a JAL flight, Makis was reminiscing about the lovely weekend he had had with Athina and her brother. He also remembered the argument about women not being the ideal persons to deal with the complicated problems of double-skin tankers, pollution etc., and how much Athina had objected to his attitude. Anyway, he thought, he should be careful in future because Athina was not just any girl.

In Yokohama, he faced a serious problem with the bulk carrier, which was to pass a Special Survey. The ultrasound measurements showed a rather serious diminution of thickness in some of the transverse bulkheads, and also in the frames of the side ballast tanks. The class surveyor calculated that they needed renewals of about 2,000 tons steel weight. This would have taken one month to complete and cost over five or six million dollars.

He had a lot of communications and discussions with a reliable shipyard in Shanghai, and after a few days he ordered the ship to go there for her repairs at an agreed cost of three million dollars and twenty-five days' completion;

and on top, the Chinese agreed to give a good penalty clause for non-performance of the job of completing repairs etc.

He gave the supervision job to another of their engineers who was already in Shanghai. So Makis stayed in Japan to take care of the sea trials of the first double-skin VLCC they were building.

The sea trials were successful, although the weather was bad and for a while there was doubt as to whether they would carry out the trials. Late in the evening, however, the wind subsided and next morning they started at 0600 and with good visibility everything was finished by 1930 hrs.

★

The meeting in Washington DC had just started. The room was full of important people; senior members of the Party, the member representing the majority in the Senate and also the Chairman of the Foreign Affairs Committee, several Governors and of course the most important person, Governor Bryant, who was the Party's candidate in the coming Presidential Elections.

The Senator, who was representing the Majority in the Senate, started.

'Gentlemen, the Party and all of us are facing a very serious problem. I will not go into the details of the matter because you all know that Governor Bryant, who is our chosen candidate to represent us in the Presidential Elections, did... well, he was involved in a stupid, farcical affair, and he let himself be the victim of a serious intrigue, which may cost us the Presidency. I would like to hear views from all of you, as to what we should do.

'We have two options, in my opinion: first, we decide to put up a new candidate and tell the people that for health or family reasons their chosen candidate, Governor Bryant, cannot stand. We propose Mr X...

'The other option we have is to silence the rumours, disregard everything and continue as before with the same candidate. Governor Bryant, very fairly and gallantly, has decided to leave the decision to us today. A decision must be taken today, simply because there is no time, no time to play around. We have, however, whatever we decide, to go all out and campaign with all our brains, all our strength and all our money, for that matter.'

A young Senator from Texas said, 'We cannot afford to go to the elections with this candidate. We are not sure, but I strongly suspect that the opposition would do anything to discredit Governor Bryant and snatch the initiative, and of course, win the election.

'The Gallup polls give us at this moment a 3% margin, and we do not want to lose it. So I move for ditching the present candidate and choosing a new one, without blemish, without a history of problems, preferably someone young and preferably from a Southern State, where we have a small weakness in accordance with the Gallup polls.'

The Senator leading the Majority of the House took the stand and said, 'What our young Senator from Texas is proposing is rather dangerous. First of all, we do not know what the opponents have on Governor Bryant. But even if we believe the worst, a serious situation can always be explained. The Governor could even go to the people himself and explain. The people may feel sympathetic, they may even feel that they should give him the benefit of the doubt. The people may even feel, "Okay, we have a president who has a weakness, a weakness which was pumped up by the opposition". I propose to you that we should continue with Governor Bryant and take steps to minimise the damage.'

The Senator from Texas was not convinced. He asked to be heard again. 'This is a serious weakness we are talking about. Some time ago there was a problem with a young

Mexican girl, a girl practically under age, and our Governor had sexual relations with her. He got out of trouble with difficulty, and by paying money.

'Now it is a nice-looking little French girl, a Lolita type, and straightaway our candidate takes her to the pool of his country house and he is probably photographed embracing her or kissing her while she was naked. No! I say no. The opponents will make a big issue of this and I do not blame them.'

An elderly Senator who was the most senior member of the Party spoke last.

'I have heard all your views. You are all right. You all have a valid point of view, but at the same time we have to make a final decision today. I agree that we have no time to lose. I realise that this matter… this action of our good Governor Bryant, who we all voted and elected to represent us in the coming elections, was bad, very bad – simply because the other side can make a big issue of it. But I feel very strongly that the electorate will smell something foul, something sinister if we tell them that the candidate we so strongly supported in the Primaries and at the Convention, is now withdrawing because of … because of *bad health.*

'Franklin D Roosevelt was elected President twice while he was suffering from a very serious disease, and he was in a wheelchair. Indeed, he went to Potsdam and Berlin and Yalta in a wheelchair.

'I strongly feel that we should keep supporting Governor Bryant, I feel we should play it quiet and pretend nothing happened, and at the same time find out how much the opposition know, what are they prepared to do about it, and most important of all, prepare for the Governor to approach the people to give them his views, his explanation – even to the extent of going to the people to apologise or ask them forgiveness; because after all, he did not *harm* the little girl. He was not caught out in bed in a remote motel. He was in his home, with a bodyguard, and the girl was set up to entrap him.'

The Senator stopped for a few minutes and then he sat down, feeling rather tired. He got up again and said, by way of conclusion, 'Let us hear some more opinions, but I give us one hour; after that we should decide.'

Several members of the Party spoke but it was obvious, at the end of the day, that the majority were in favour of keeping the status quo and retaining the Governor as the Party's official candidate.

Finally, Governor Bryant spoke. 'I am sorry about what has happened. I am sure it was all a set-up, but I promise to you that if you decide to maintain the situation as it is for the coming elections, I will do my damnedest to campaign so that we have a good chance of winning, and I pledge two million dollars of my personal wealth to go towards the election campaign.'

The young Senator from Texas spoke last.

'I will abide by the decision of the majority today, but I want it mentioned in the minutes of today's conference that my opinion was different. I insist on this.'

The newspapers in the course of the whole week were full of the news. They were not precise as to what happened, but there was a strong insinuation that something sinister, something vaguely serious was in the air, something to do with the Presidential Elections, and especially with the candidate of one Party, the one that showed a small majority in the Gallup polls.

One of the newspapers went as far as suggesting that there was a rumour that the candidate for President would possibly resign. But there was no confirmation from any serious source.

There was even some discussion at the ladies' afternoon tea held for the Charity of Christ meeting. The Governor's wife was presiding, and one lady who was constantly raising problems and questions asked, 'Can the Chairperson tell us whether there is any substance to the rumours that the Presidential Candidate is likely to resign? And if it is true, what are the real reasons for such resignation?'

Although the wife was taken by surprise, she got up and said, 'No, there's no truth in the rumours. No. My husband is still the Party's candidate for the Presidential Elections, and he is confident that he will win.'

It was finally decided. The wedding of Makis to Athina would take place on November 5th at the Greek Orthodox Cathedral in New York. The Archbishop would officiate, and there would be representatives from the clergy and of course the families of both the bride and groom, members of the shipping company and friends.

The only difficulty with this arrangement and the date chosen was Senator Michael Glinos. It was the date of the Presidential Election, but the Senator, after a lot of thinking and deliberations, decided to be there at the wedding, to give the bride away – his beloved daughter, Athina.

The reception was arranged to take place at the country home of Makis' parents, outside New York on the way to La Rochelle.

Makis was just back from Yokohama, and as he listened to all the detailed arrangements he was absolutely fed up. His mind was dazed listening to flower arrangements, materials and lighting and sound arrangements.

He said to the man in charge of practically everything that it was better and simpler when he was in dry dock doing a Special Survey of a VLCC.

'What does VLCC stands for?' Athina had asked him one day long time ago.

'Very large crude carrier,' he replied.

'Honey, of course I know what VLCC stands for!' Athina had said, with a little anger in her voice.

There was a big meeting of the Party organisation in Washington. Senator Michael Glinos started speaking in a rather subdued voice.

'Gentlemen, it appears that the opposition is well and truly down. They are crumbling. It appears that photographers snapped the good Governor in some extremely compromising position with a little girl, with a Lolita, a very young girl who was practically naked. She was embracing the good Governor, and you know where? By the pool at his country house. There was nobody else present.

'As you know, little girls – little students – have always been the weakness of "his Lordship".

'There was an event a few years ago, a rather dirty, dark event that had to be taken care of by the family and I understand some money changed hands...

'So, gentlemen, we have to be careful. We have to wait for developments, and be aware in case we have to get our political machine moving.'

'We must now show that we can initiate or organise something against the opposition, in case the people think that we are responsible for the downfall of the Governor.' He paused and looked around the room.

'I think we can always leak information and bad rumours to one of our newspapers,' one of the young campaign organisers said. 'We can even buy space in one of the fashion magazines and in one of the Manhattan financial publications.'

'No, no!' insisted the Senator. 'We must not appear to have precipitated this scandal. It may count against us. It may ruin us if we are not careful!'

Anyway, at the end of the meeting, the Senator's opinion

prevailed, and it was decided that they should wait for developments, especially from the Governor's camp, where they were losing ground all the time.

★

In a small provincial town in Nevada, the editor of the local newspaper, the *Gazette*, was still in the office at eight p.m. He was rather depressed, because lately things were not going well for the paper. He had built the publication up from nothing; he'd worked hard the last five years, introduced new methods and new technology in the printing section, but still, what news could you expect from little town with just 20,000 inhabitants? There were no scandals, no terrorists, no rape or other crimes, or any other 'modern' event. The only excitement came once in a few years when there was a strike in the local plastics factory. Anyway, the editor was still living there; he had raised a family, he was satisfied because every Saturday he played his poker game with his friends; and once a month, secretly, without any discussion, he went to a nearby town, where he visited the well-equipped brothel. He was well known there and the owner, an old French lady over seventy years of age, was ready to provide him with the best talent.

But that particular evening, the editor was depressed. He even thought of closing down the little newspaper. He had some money saved. He was well off, not a rich man but well off.

There was a soft knock on the door. Who could it be at that late hour of the evening? The 'CLOSED' sign was on the door, but still, the knock was persistent.

He went to the door and saw a nicely-dressed young lady who said, 'I have some very important, juicy gossip, which I think you would definitely like to print in your *Gazette*. It has something to do with the upcoming Presidential Elections, and...'

'I am not interested in wild gossip, young lady, and I certainly do not intend to go to prison in my old age!' And while saying this, the editor started pushing at the door, effectively pushing the young lady out. He realised that she had her foot inside the door and would not let go. He realised that she meant business, but of course, he did not want to be involved in something sinister or something intriguing and possibly untrue.

'Look, just listen to me for two minutes,' the lady said. 'I have a terrific story that has to do with one of the candidates. I have photographs, I have the works.' She stopped for a moment and then continued. 'If you print the story and a few photographs, you will be famous within a day. You will be the talk of Washington DC and you can sell the story and the photos for a million dollars easy, to start with. To you it will only cost 100,000 dollars, and I promise you that with TV rights and press rights, etc., you will gross at least five million dollars...'

'Thank you, but go away. I am not interested.'

'Okay. I am going, but I will come back in two days' time. The same time, the same place. I will give you a sample of what I have so that you can judge yourself. But remember, you must have 100,000 dollars.'

'Where would I get 100,000 dollars for your sort of crap? Anyway, let me have the "sample", as you call it.'

The lady gave the editor an envelope and disappeared into the night.

The old editor had heard these things before. The TV stories were full of it. He had heard of intrigues, political blackmail and all the rest of it; but of course it was all in his imagination, and nobody knew the source of these events. He also knew that a lot of money could be made with these scandals, especially political scandals. Maybe he was naive. Maybe he was ignorant. He decided anyway that he did not really wish to get involved.

When he got home that night, he went straight to his little den. His wife was surprised, because for the first time in over forty years, he had few words for her. Usually they had a nice conversation before he disappeared into his den.

'Anything wrong, dear?' she asked.

'No, no, I am busy. I have to check on something. So nothing unusual. I do not understand it, dear. I simply do not understand it.' And saying these last words, he disappeared into the den.

He put on the light, then he switched on the heavy floodlight and he even closed and locked the door of the den. He opened the envelope that the young lady had given him and took a magnifying glass out of the drawer. He was agitated, and in a way he was upset.

In front of him he had two not very good photographs and a page of typewritten story. In the photographs he immediately recognised the likeness of the Governor who was the presidential candidate in the forthcoming elections. He was wearing only swimming trunks and he had in his arms a very young girl, a girl who seemed to be barely sixteen. She was also in a swimming costume; in fact she was wearing a topless swimming costume.

The typewritten page went as follows:

Is this the man we want to rule us? Is this the man who will be the leader of the free world? We are proud of our country, we are proud of our heritage, but with this man at the top, we will be ashamed to confront the world.

He put the photographs in the envelope. Then he opened a small safe that was hidden behind a painting on the wall, stored the envelope, locked the safe and went back to join his wife. He asked her for a stiff brandy and sat down on his special rocking chair.

His wife now knew there was something wrong, or at

least, that something was bothering her husband.

After drinking his brandy, the editor could not keep the problem in any longer. He went to the armchair where his wife of forty years was sitting and told her slowly but clearly what had happened in the office. He told her all about the photographs and the terrible implication that this scandal could have for the coming elections, for the people and also for the whole structure of society.

'So what do I do now?' he asked her.

She was standing now, holding his hand and said, 'This is a very great problem; too great and serious for you to bear, my love. I think that you should ask or seek the opinion of our friend Senator Barret, and also speak to your brother, who is involved in serious politics. They can give you their opinions and after you get their views, then... then we can discuss this matter and you and I will decide. As always, we will decide.'

'I think you are right. They will be able to tell me a few things, especially Frank, my brother, who is also involved in our small printing and editing business.'

While this conversation was taking place, the same lady who had been to the office of the provincial newspaper and handed the 'sample' to the editor was in a telephone booth and was talking to somebody abroad. She had placed a collect call international, and was waiting for a response.

'Hello, hello? It's all done. The editor was in two minds about what to do, but finally he took the envelope with the sample of two photos... What do you want me to do now?' she asked, after listening to someone on the other side of the Atlantic.

'Okay then. In that case, I shall expect to find 100,000 US dollars in my account in Switzerland. I have given you the number, but... you have to be prompt, not like last time. You must be exact, as I am exact and I perform. Do you have any complaints? Of course you don't!' She paused. 'Okay. Thanks. And make sure the money is there at ten o'clock tomorrow morning.'

Eight

Shadow Play

November 5th was approaching fast.

Two great events were happening in the family of Senator Michael Glinos, and he was sincerely hoping that both would be *happy* occasions.

The wedding preparations were proceeding very fast. A firm specialising in catering and decorations was engaged at a high cost and they were making a mess of the garden, front and back, where Makis' parents lived. They were really very quiet people, and not very sociable. But now it was a great occasion, and they were happy that Athina's family had agreed that the reception would take place with floral decorations and arches so that no one could recognise the house.

Of course Makis' family started worrying about expenses, until Makis calmed his father and mother down and told them that it was being taken care of.

One day, Makis' father saw in his garden a huge sawing machine, ready to cut down the two conifers of which he was so proud. He stopped the operation just in time; but the 'General' – he called him a general – the man in charge of the operation told him that the trees would have to go so that they could build floral arches there. However, after the wedding they would plant some special species which grew quickly, and they would grow to the same height as his own two conifers within three years.

And at the same time, there was a lot of work and never ending meetings and canvassing efforts in the campaign central office of the Party, where Senator Michael Glinos was conducting all operations of his presidential campaign.

A serious problem was cost, because the initial budget had been $20 million, and this amount was collected from sponsors and members of the Party, and also from parties and dinners which were done for a fundraising effort.

There was a highly important meeting that evening and only the top officials would attend: three senior Senators, four elderly Governors and a dozen Party members who had contributed substantially for the election campaign. The Senator, the candidate, was not present as he had to attend another meeting of the Defense Department, but his top aide opened the proceedings.

'Gentlemen, we have to decide on one important issue. The candidate of the opposite side, Governor Bryant, has a serious problem, which in my opinion could lose him the Presidency. He was caught a couple of weeks ago, at his poolside in Connecticut, holding in his arms a very young girl, and they were kissing. He was in his swimming trunks and the Lolita was practically naked. She was topless. As you know, the Governor had a similar incident in this field with a very young Mexican girl. At the time he got out of it, but it is well known that a lot of money changed hands.

'We also know that a provincial newspaper editor was approached by a person, an unknown person, and was given a set of photos showing the Governor holding the young, half-naked girl at the poolside; this unknown person will give the editor these photos and demands 100,000 dollars.

'Of course, these photos and the scandal could bring this poor newspaper editor, who has been struggling for the last three to four years, over a million dollars. The man has not yet made a decision whether to publish the photos. I understand that he wants to consult a certain Senator who is a friend of his, also his brother… but… but I can assure you that both the Senator and the brother are "kindly" disposed to our side.'

He stopped for a while, drank some water, wiped his forehead and continued, 'During the previous meeting when this idea was discussed, we did not know the exact details and what exactly these photos showed, and it was decided that we should not push the matter, that we should not reveal ourselves as being the initiators of the scandal.

'However, now a third person is involved: the editor of a provincial newspaper, who could – if we play our cards right – publish the story and blow up any chances our opponent has of winning the Election, in spite of the 3% lead he has. I now want to hear your views, but all I wish to add is that there is no time to waste, and the 3% lead has been there for over three months and has not altered at all. Of course, one has to be extremely careful about using this unexpected good fortune, so that we can be sure of success.'

There was a very strong discussion, with very bitter feelings exposed on either side, because there were a couple of old Party faithful members who insisted that this was not fair dealing, and that people may accuse their side of a bad, twisted approach to the campaign for the Presidency. One of the members even felt that some people might think that the Governor was terrific because he had managed to attract a very young girl – he was a great 'macho man'.

At the end of the meeting, they practically all agreed that the only chance they had of overtaking the 3% was to allow the publication of the story and the revealing photos. Because after all, the most senior members present said, 'This is pornography, this is paedophiliac action, and the Governor has done it before and he should not get away with it. Anyway, we cannot possibly have a President of our country who has such a weakness.'

'So we all agree! No more arguments! We let things run their course. We will not interfere ourselves; not obviously, anyway. We will continue our campaign as strongly as we can and we shall use our last dollar in order to succeed, but if the papers publish the story of our "famous" Governor with the little girl, then... then the people themselves will not vote for him.

'Any questions? Any objections?'

Nobody said anything and the meeting was over. They all went out, some smiling, some apprehensive, and one or two really worried.

A few days before the Presidential Elections, in the small town in Nevada, the local newspaper was suddenly in great demand. From seven in the morning, people were queuing outside the little offices in order to secure a few copies of the local *Gazette*.

The owner and his son, together with hired help, stayed up all night in order to be able to print the scandalous story, print the photographs and make sure that the details were not in any way libellous or incorrect.

About noon, they had to prepare for a second edition because the first lot was exhausted within three hours of publication.

The telephone lines never stopped humming, and there were even calls from Washington DC, from the FBI, the CIA, and even several Congressmen called the editor, who could not answer further questions. Finally, towards the evening, he decided to disappear to his home, although even there, there was no peace.

Late at night the threats started coming through: threats from individuals, from politicians, from the police; so after a while, the editor had to refer everything to his attorneys. The attorneys had done their homework well, working carefully so that there was no fear of being accused of libel or other unheard-of offences.

The man was exhausted. In his forty years as an editor on the *Gazette*, he had never seen so much commotion, he never had so much notoriety; and of course all of a sudden he felt important. Important in the sense that his newspaper went further than publishing for the local school and the local brewery. He was printing for the nation. He was influencing the vote of the population for the forthcoming Presidential Elections.

He did not know where the $100,000 came from for the payment of the photographs to the young lady who had called at the editor's office. He did not know who paid it. He knew it was paid. He also knew that there were three offers from international organisations of one million dollars each for the story and for the exclusive presentation of the whole thing.

One thing worried him, though. He received a phone call late at night, near midnight, and the person who spoke to him was very clear:

'You will not live to enjoy this action of yours. You will regret it, you see. You and your family.'

Next morning, the local Sheriff spoke to him, and without asking questions, he appointed one of his best detectives outside the house and another young detective outside the newspaper offices. 'For your personal protection,' he told him. 'I have definite instructions from New York.'

★

On November 2nd, Makis and Athina, together with some members of the family, went to the Greek Cathedral in downtown New York in order to do a rehearsal of the wedding ceremony.

The best man was present, and a few friends from the shipping company. It appeared that Makis was not very used to the Greek liturgy, and he was also slightly ignorant of the actual ceremony, so he had to be taught everything from the beginning.

Athina was brought in by her brother, who deputised for the Senator; he in turn had to be at the campaign headquarters in Washington DC.

It was a tedious ceremony which had to be repeated several times until all the participants got everything right.

The Bishop and the priest, Father Robert, were of course at their best and they corrected everybody to the complete satisfaction of the aunts and uncles, who were following all the proceedings with a critical eye.

They were now outside the church, and as Athina was coming down the steps, a man approached her, a vicious-looking, swarthy man with an Arab complexion. He gave her a small envelope, and before she or Makis, who was standing by, had time to stop him or ask who he was, he disappeared into the crowd. He got on a powerful motorcycle, whose engine was left running, and he was off.

Makis took the small envelope from Athina, and before opening it he smelt it, then brought it to his ears to check whether there was some sort of sinister mechanism inside. Then he took from it a piece of dirty white paper with a typewritten text that read:

YOU WILL NOT GET MARRIED TO THE TRAITOR OF THE TALEBAN CAUSE.

This piece of paper was given to the agent of the FBI who was with them. He arranged to have double security for both Athina and Makis straight away.

The next morning, the Senator phoned Makis at home and told him that there was a suspicion that this frantic, crazy effort to influence the wedding – and possibly the Election – did not come from the Taleban. They had traced the source to the headquarters of the Senator's opponents. They had even found the typewriter that wrote the text. It had a twisted 'T' in it, and there were a lot of 'T's in the text.

At the campaign headquarters there was a lot of excitement. The effect of the publication of the Nevada *Gazette* was electric, and news spread to the headquarters that there was a very important meeting of the opponent's top men so they could decide what to do.

There was an official declaration of the latest Gallup poll, which showed a 1½% margin for the opponents – down from 3%.

The decision at the headquarters was that they should not stop their efforts, that the campaign in all States should go on, and new finance was approved especially in the Southern States and California.

It was also decided by the committee of the top men working for the election of the Senator that a cleverly-formed article would be prepared, outlining the impropriety of their opponent, including the two cases of sexual 'adventure' with the Mexican girl and the Lolita of a few days ago; it would be given to the international press and possibly a few glossy magazines.

The next day it was learnt that the opposition camp had decided to keep their candidate, the famous Governor, and not risk a last minute change. This was the decision taken by the high elite of the Party – firstly because they could not agree on a new candidate, and secondly because they felt that the young voters might decide that the Governor was showing a strong masculine, macho image.

A last effort was then made by the campaign strategists of Senator Michael Glinos, who managed to enlist the top Church leaders, to show how decadent it would be to have as a president a man who had no concept of ethics or good behaviour, and would stoop to degrade himself with innocent little girls.

★

The wedding day of Athina and Makis finally arrived. It was a sunny morning, slightly cool, with a north wind that was rather pleasant.

There was a lot of excitement and wild activity in the campaign headquarters, at the house of Senator Michael Glinos, and everywhere else. He and his wife and son started early, heading for New York. The private plane that took them northwards set them down at a small airport near the city. Here a large limousine was waiting to take them to an apartment that they hired very near the Greek cathedral.

Athina was there, attended by her bridesmaids, her old aunt and of course the chief person in charge of decorations and the wedding dress. He was a feminine-looking individual who Makis despised enormously, but... but he was part of the 'story'.

Athina looked extremely beautiful in her wedding dress, and when her father and mother came in and saw her, she burst into tears, tears of joy. Even the Senator was not unmoved, and he wiped little tears of happiness away with his white handkerchief.

The ceremony in the cathedral was magnificent. The building was beautifully decorated with white roses and the floral arches at the entrance of the church and near the table were made of lovely white orchids. As the Senator proceeded down the church at a slow pace, holding his beloved daughter, and approached Makis, he could not keep back his tears any more. He said to himself, May God protect her and him.

The Greek Orthodox wedding ceremony was halfway through when members of the Senator's staff started coming to the church to keep him advised of developments and how the exit polls were showing.

The Senator, in spite of his efforts and will to succeed in this lifelong ambition of his, was at this moment fairly cool. His attention was given over to the wedding ceremony rather than the results of the polls in Texas, or Kentucky or Illinois.

In fact, he could not remember what his assistants were saying about which State came his way, which of the large States were won and which were lost.

His feelings were rather vague. He felt a strong feeling of happiness which probably came from the holy ceremony and the wedding vows. And all of a sudden he found himself praying, which he had not done for a long, long time.

'God Almighty, I know I have not prayed for a long time before now, I know I have done a lot of bad things in my life. God Almighty, forgive my sins and give this girl, my daughter, and her husband Your holy blessing; give them love, and love, and love. And I do not know what else to ask You.'

The wedding ceremony was now over.

They were all now going off to the house belonging to Makis' parents. The couple looked so radiant as they got into the limousine. The guests followed behind them, and after an hour's drive, they arrived at their destination. It was nearly nine o'clock.

The house and the garden looked spectacular and the lighting was most impressive. All the family were there, as well as everybody from the shipping company.

The whole Washington DC staff were present except his own men, his assistants and people who were working in the campaign headquarters and some of the staff who were spread out around the various States, supervising the election campaign.

For a single moment he thought of the Presidential Election. One of the top assistants just told him that the exit polls show a 50–50 share of the vote with a slight tendency, as the day wore on, towards the Senator.

A lot of people came to congratulate Senator Glinos and his wife on the marriage of Athina. They all wished them happiness, and as he walked inside for a moment, he saw one corner of the sitting room full of presents that people had brought and also a lot of envelopes – no doubt full of money, in the old Italian and Greek custom.

He was thinking that people's customs do not really change.

It was past midnight and the Senator saw some of the attendants wheeling in a huge wedding cake. It was so beautiful. It was in the centre of the room, and Makis and Athina were approaching the table and the cake. Suddenly the music and the noise stopped, and one of the caterers announced, 'Please, fill your glasses with champagne, to toast the newly weds, who will cut the wedding cake.'

'For Makis and Athina – happiness and health!'

The Senator approached the newlyweds, kissed them and asked whether he could say a few words.

'Ladies and gentlemen... All I wish to say is thank you all for coming today from all parts of the world to celebrate the wedding of these two young persons. I cannot say much because, I am very... very overcome with emotion. May God keep you healthy and happy.'

He put the champagne glass down as one of the assistants approached him and said, 'Mr President, congratulations on the wedding of your daughter... and Mr President, congratulations to you! It has just been announced on TV and radio.'

While they were all congratulating the President and the newlyweds, there was a telephone call from London. Captain Bob took it and the English broker told him to ask Makis to phone the seller of the *Dream Come True* in Stavanger, Norway, urgently.

He did not wish to interrupt Makis' happiness with business, but he also knew that if the phone call had anything to do with the ship that Makis was after, he could tell him.

Makis took the phone in the small room near the kitchen.

'Mr Makis? I am Mr Morinsen, from Stavanger, the owner of the *Gianbattista* – the 40,0000-tonner you are after.'

Makis felt his heart stopping. 'Okay, Mr Makis, I will accept your price and terms, and I will give you 70% credit because I know that you come from a seafaring family like me. The ship is yours. We will deliver it in Rotterdam on completion of discharge of her coal cargo. Now, Mr Makis what are you going to call your first ship?'

'*Pallas* or *Athina* – and thank you, sir, thank you! I have two happy events today. I've just got married to a wonderful girl, and I've just bought my first ship!'

And with this, he put the phone down and rushed off to find Athina.

'Good news about the new ship! She will be called *Pallas* or *Athina*. It is all confirmed.'

'God protect us,' said Athina. 'Too many happy things happened today.'

★

On the same quiet Greek island, the one with the small whitewashed church, it was winter time, just before Christmas. The little church was somehow freshly painted and repaired.

It was late afternoon. A chris-craft with one man aboard appeared and moored in a little wooded inlet.

A man got out and went towards the church. He held a high-powered VHF telephone. He sat outside the church and made three telephone calls. With some difficulty he managed to get through. The conversation was the same in each case.

'I wish to report to No.1 that the decisions which were made in this location 360 days ago, were successfully carried out.'

CPSIA information can be obtained
at www.ICGtesting.com
Printed in the USA
LVHW040413201218
601074LV00001BB/86/P

9 781844 013159